Tiberius wiped the  **then slid it over his bare chest. The whi... soaked up the sweat rolling down his** ~~body~~

As though she were in a daze, Capri walked up behind him and reached out. Tiberius jerked around when he felt the towel being pulled from his hands. The furrow on his brow vanished when he saw Capri. Speechless, his eyes followed her every move.

Capri completed the task of wiping the sweat away from Tiberius's body. Her dark stare followed the towel's path over the chiseled expanse of his back. Gathering her robe from around her ankles, she stepped in front of Tiberius and knelt before him. She favored his wide chest with the same smooth strokes as his back.

Satisfied with the results, she set the towel aside and began pressing soft kisses to the bulging pectorals that contracted beneath her touch. As her soft lips trailed downward across his solid abs, Tiberius leaned his head back and groaned. When Capri's soft caress continued its path downward, Tiberius's eyes snapped open and he grabbed her upper arms.

"Capri, do you know what you're doing?" he asked, his voice raspy with desire.

Capri's doe-eyed gaze was unwavering. "I want you. I want to make love with you."

"I hope you mean that. I'm not in the mood to be teased right now."

"I'm not teasing, I want this," she said softly, sincerely.

"I only want you to do this if you're certain," Tiberius warned her. He didn't want her having any doubts.

Capri kept her dark gaze focused on his warm brown one. Untying her robe's belt, she pushed the silky material away from her body. "I'm certain."

Books by AlTonya Washington

Kimani Romance	Kimani Arabesque
A Lover's Pretense	*Remember Love*
A Lover's Mask	*Guarded Love*
Pride and Consequence	*Finding Love Again*
Rival's Desire	*Love Scheme*
Hudsons Crossing	*A Lover's Dream*
The Doctor's Private Visit	

ALTONYA WASHINGTON

has been a published romance novelist for six years. Her novel *Finding Love Again* won the *RT Book Reviews* Reviewer's Choice Award for Best Multicultural Romance in 2004. In addition to teaching a community college course entitled *Writing the Romance Novel,* she works as a Senior Library Assistant and resides in North Carolina. AlTonya released her fifteenth novel, *Hudsons Crossing,* in March 2009.

AlTONYA WASHINGTON

The
Doctor's
Private Visit

KIMANI
ROMANCE

To those who've dared to flirt on the most
delicious sides of temptation.

 KIMANI PRESS™

ISBN-13: 978-0-373-86146-0

Recycling programs
for this product may
not exist in your area.

THE DOCTOR'S PRIVATE VISIT

Copyright © 2010 by AlTonya Washington

www.kimanipress.com

Printed in U.S.A.

Dear Reader,

The Doctor's Private Visit is a provocative story that I hope you'll find as pleasurable to read as it was for me to write. Photographer Capri Timmons and Dr. Tiberius Evans rival their Miami setting for heat and allure.

While crafting this tale, the word *temptation* frequently came to mind. And it's the sheer force of temptation between Capri and Tiberius that relentlessly beckons them to give in to all their delicious and unexpected desires.

Feel free to let me know your thoughts on this latest effort. E-mail me at altonya@lovealtonya.com, and visit my Web site at www.lovealtonya.com to keep up on all my projects, including the sequel to last year's Kimani Romance release, *Hudsons Crossing*.

Be blessed,

AlTonya

Chapter 1

Capri Timmons lay back on the gray suede couch and threw her shapely legs across the arm. She toyed with a lock of her curly, baby-fine hair, sighed, and tossed about impatiently.

Roderick Jackson glanced up but tried to keep his attention on the glossy proof sheet lying on his desk. When Capri uttered another heavy sigh, Rod rolled his eyes toward her and shook his head. Tightening his grip on the huge magnifying glass in his hand, he tried once more to concentrate.

Capri began humming a monotonous tune that sounded like a cat gurgling in a bucket of water. Rod gave up all hope of reviewing the proof sheet. He glared across his office at the petite caramel-colored beauty lounging on his sofa. "Something on your mind, Cappy?"

"Uh-uh," Capri denied absently.

The look in Rod's slanting coal-black eyes clearly stated he wasn't buying it. Since he knew the strikingly beautiful thirty-one-year-old well, he waited for her to speak up.

"In the meantime," he murmured, reaching for the portfolio lying on the opposite end of the sofa, "make yourself useful." He tossed the leather-bound tote to Capri. "Jerard's proofs," he explained when she studied him. "We need to pick his best shots for the *Miami Hoods* cover."

Capri's face glossed over with a bright expression. "I know he's on pins and needles about this," she sighed, referring to her newest colleague who had just scored his first photo spread.

Capri dove into the task and an easy silence settled between her and Roderick for the better part of thirty minutes. Scanning the gorgeous shots of some of Miami's most elaborate dwellings, however, Capri couldn't help but throw thought to her current issue.

"I don't think I'll be much help here, Rod. These places are… incredible, all of them."

Low chuckling rose from the other side of the bright, chic office. "That's why I didn't bother taking them home. Kiva would have a fit drooling over the damn things." He paused to make a notation regarding one of Capri's shots. "All I'd hear is how she'd give her left arm to have a place like that," he continued.

Capri shared in the chuckling. "I know how she feels. And that's in spite of the fact that you guys have your own palace already," she was referring to Rod and Kiva's home in Braxton Hills, one of Miami's most impressive neighborhoods.

"Oh yeah." Rod's attention was still quite focused on the work before him, "I remember Ki saying something about your thoughts on Miami life."

"Mmm, did she tell you everything I said?" Capri's gaze was focused on Jerard's shots as she spoke.

"Just about," he said as he slanted her a wicked glance. "When you've got lots of drama-queen friends, sharing can't be helped, you know?" A grin crossed his handsome face when Capri tossed a wad of paper at his forehead.

Capri propped herself up on her elbows as she lay flat on her stomach. "It's just starting to wear me out mentally, you know? Living *and* working here. I guess I'm just craving a little distance in between."

Rod scratched his dark, short hair and nodded. "Yeah, I can understand that, but I hope you don't start to think about leaving Miami permanently."

Capri sat up in the middle of the sofa and tucked her legs beneath her. "No, no, that's not it," she firmly assured Rod. "But I could see myself selling the condo for something…"

"Less city," Rod finished for her.

"Crazy, huh?"

Rod shrugged. "I expect nothin' less from a drama queen."

After a moment, the two old friends burst into peals of laughter. Of course, Capri couldn't totally deny that she had a wonderful home. Working for Grant and Shields Photography studio had earned both her and Rod respect in their field, not to mention incomes that would raise more than a few eyebrows.

Rod was one of the head directors of photography. Capri had interned for him when she was in college and he'd just been hired at the studio. The two became fast friends and a romance had never sparked between them because Rod always thought of Capri as a little sister. In turn, Capri loved him like the brother she'd missed out on having as the youngest of four girls.

"Let me see if I can get this straight." Rod sighed, when his laughter had somewhat subsided. "You're tired of city-living in condos and now you want a house?"

Capri trailed her fingers through her curly bob and winced. "I hadn't really thought of a *house* per se, just something a bit off the beaten track." Her dark gaze shimmered then. "A home of my own would be…wonderful."

Rod leaned back in his chair and stroked the light beard that shadowed his face. "I just might be able to help."

Capri's eyes widened like a child's in a toy store. "You could?"

"Now, don't get all excited, but I know a doctor who rents out homes surrounding his estate."

Impressed, Capri's arched brows rose slightly. "How do you know somebody like that?"

Rod shrugged. "We grew up together."

"Uh-huh," Capri grunted suspiciously, knowing there was a lot more to the simple statement. "What? Does he own the entire neighborhood or something?"

"No, Cappy," Rod assured her, chuckling softly, "but, his

grandmother just about had the whole thing under her thumb. She died and left the main house and four homes surrounding it to her grandson. Think you might be interested if I could set it up?"

Capri rested back on her heels and mulled over the offer. She thought about the pros and cons of living in a large fast-paced city, as compared to having her own private oasis miles away. She recalled Rod saying this doctor friend of his *rented*. While not having ownership of the property she'd reside in gave her pause, she believed she could set that aside for the moment. A change of pace, scenery and a bit more breathing room for a year or so could possibly do wonders for her current outlook.

"All right folks, if that's all, we'll see each other for next week's meeting on Wednesday at two o'clock sharp." Dr. Oscar Addison stood before his obstetrics staff and watched his doctors and nurses vacate the conference room amidst the familiar rumble of laughter and chatter.

Nurses Avra Vickers and Sandy Weisbeck cornered Dr. Tiberius Evans before he left through the room's side entrance.

"We're still waiting for confirmation on that invite to our housewarming, Tibe."

"Right." Tiberius sighed, his mouth curving in an apologetic smile as he remembered the date and the fact that he'd been hoping it would pass without the nurses recalling the invitation.

Avra rolled her eyes toward Sandy. "I can see a 'sorry ladies but I'm afraid...' coming on."

Sandy added, "What's going on now, Tibe? Don't you realize we haven't hung out together in...*damn,* way too long?"

Tiberius rested a hand across his white coat. "I've just got a lot going on around here, that's all."

"Well!" Sandy pretended to be exasperated as she clapped a hand to her cheek. "Av, I do believe I'm offended. Is the good doctor saying that *we* don't have a lot going on around here, too?"

"Mmm-hmm, I do believe that's what he's trying to say, Sand." Avra's lashes fluttered.

"Don't do this to me, y'all."

"Then just come."

"In every way." Wicked intent flooded Sandy's brown eyes with more sparkle.

Tiberius could only chuckle at their determination.

"Seriously, Tibe, you know that we'll show you a fantastic time."

Sandy mimicked her roommate's pleading expression. "Remember our last housewarming?"

Nodding, Tiberius rubbed his fingers through his silky curls and envisioned the long-ago romp with the two uninhibited RNs.

"Will you settle for me saying I'll see what I can do?"

Avra clapped her hands while Sandy clenched a triumphant fist. They decided to leave before he turned them down flat.

"Oh, to be young again," Oscar Addison sang from his position at the head of the long table across the room.

Grinning, Tiberius slapped his palm against the side of his portfolio and turned back toward his older colleague. "It's not all it's cracked up to be, Doc."

"Is that cynicism I hear in your voice, young man?"

Tiberius laughed out loud. "More than a little bit."

Oscar smoothed the back of his hand across the beard shadowing his dark face. "Aren't you a little young to be so jaded?"

"I don't think you can ever be too young to latch on to good sense, Doc."

Curious now, Oscar Addison perched on one corner of the pine table with its rows of stout brass-toned lamps. "No, you're never too young for good sense, but I'd have to disagree as it relates to using all your considerable charms on a very willing opposite sex."

"Well I'd say you've got quite a bit of charm left yourself."

Tiberius noted, grinning at the doctor he'd known since his early days of residency at Kelly Memorial.

Dr. Oscar Addison had a charismatic demeanor which was as effective on his patients as it was on his staff. In spite of the love and admiration he drew from people like water from a well, he handled it all with a humbleness that Tiberius thoroughly respected.

"You're damn right, and I use it every chance I get." Oscar began to scratch at the gray just starting to sprinkle his beard. "Used it more when I had youth to back it up."

Tiberius opted for a spot on the other end of the table. "I don't think age plays such a huge factor. Look at Dr. T—he's still kickin' and he's way older than you."

Oscar nodded, his expression brightening at the thought of his beloved mentor Alan Thomas. "There's exceptions to every rule. Speaking of Dr. T, there's something I wanted to run past you."

Tiberius set his portfolio on the table and waited. "Somethin' wrong?"

"Have you heard about Alan's retirement?" Oscar pulled the black-rimmed spectacles from his face and eased them inside the front pocket of the denim shirt beneath his coat.

"I was hoping it was a joke." Tiberius shrugged. "But at seventy-one, I guess the man's got a right."

"I think so, but before Dr. Alan Thomas leaves, we want to send him off in style and give him a retirement gala he won't forget."

Tiberius nodded slowly. "Excellent idea."

"Glad you think so," Oscar said as he pushed off the table. "We want you in charge of the memories portion of the event."

"The...what?"

"Memories, Tiberius. Walking down memory lane?" Oscar added for clarification. "You can choose your own committee, handle it with your own style, but we want to see something that commemorates the man's career. Perhaps a memory book presented to him at the end of the night, filled with little notes of well-wishes signed by the staff, past colleagues and what have you. Maybe you could combine that with some sort of roast."

"Good ideas, Doc. But do you really want *me* overseeing this?"

"That's why it *has* to be you." Oscar chuckled through the words. "You'll get the job done in a professional manner just to be rid of it and you won't waste time bickering over petty nonsense."

Tiberius's handsome face was a study in shock as he listened to Oscar Addison discussing ideas for meetings, choosing the committee and everything else involved in planning the surprise.

"I'd hope you'll have chosen your team by the first meeting. But the thing's scheduled several months out, so there's time." Grabbing his paperwork, Oscar clapped Tiberius's shoulder. "Perk up, I'm sure any of the nurses would be pleased to work on the project with you."

Tiberius responded with a knowing smirk. "Thanks, Doc."

Roderick smiled and nodded while holding his office door open for Capri. "Cappy, this is Avery Erickson. Ave, this is Capri Timmons."

Avery's dark eyes lit up as they appraised Capri's face and petite, curvaceous form. "Damn, man, you mean to tell me you get to work with this lady every day?" he questioned in playful disbelief.

Rod chuckled. "I do."

Avery shook his head and turned to Capri. Taking her by the hand, he stared right into her doe eyes. "It's nice to meet you, Ms. Timmons, and let me just say that you are incredibly beautiful."

Capri smiled and cut her gaze to Rod who was enjoying seeing her experience a rare case of embarrassment. "Thank you, but please call me Capri."

Avery dipped his head. "And please call me Avery."

Rod rolled his eyes at his friend and sighed. "Man, please stop this act. You know you work around hundreds of beautiful women all the time."

Avery never took his eyes from Capri. "Never any this beautiful," he replied.

The last thing Capri wanted to do was laugh in the face of the man who'd been chosen to do a series of spreads for the studio preparing a new men's fragrance. Instead, she smiled and coolly extracted her hand from Avery's grasp. Walking closer to Rod's desk, she sat down and gave him a look that demanded he start the meeting immediately.

"Well, Avery," Rod called, rubbing his hands together, "I'm glad you find Capri so appealing, since she's the photographer in charge of the shoot."

"You're kidding," Avery blurted, taking a seat and propping his face in his palm.

Capri smoothed her hands over her cream-colored coat dress and recrossed her legs. "Is that a problem?"

"No, ma'am." Avery frowned. "Not at all. I'm just surprised to see such a young lovely woman in charge of the shoot."

Rod cast a quick glance in Capri's direction and could tell that she wasn't satisfied with that answer. Rushing to keep the waters calm, he cleared his throat. "We chose Capri because of her expertise with the nude layouts she frequently produces for several well-known women's magazines. Haize Fragrances, the company that created the cologne, loves her work, too, so, of course she was the obvious choice."

"Will you have a problem working with me, Avery?" Capri asked again, not wanting to waste any more time than necessary with the man.

"I won't, Capri. You're the boss," Avery assured her.

"Well, will you have a problem working in the bare minimum?"

"None."

Capri nodded and reached for the portfolio on Rod's desk. "All right, well, since the cologne created by Haize Fragrances is called Bare Minimum, I think the shots should reflect that very idea. I want to set up shoots in different locations void of lots of props and extras. For instance, in a light, airy room, furnished with only a chair or a lamp. Or say by the beach with maybe a palm tree far in the background," she explained, shifting in her seat. "See, I want the shots showing the least of everything, no matter what the setting, with a few shots of you in nice suits for good measure."

Avery and Rod nodded in unison. Capri smiled and opened her portfolio. "If you gentlemen will gather around, I can show you the visuals for the location my crew and I have decided on."

"Droopey? Droopey! Come on!" Tiberius glanced at his watch as he held one of the doors open on his truck.

In a few seconds, a gorgeous female collie raced out to the driveway. At her master's request, she hopped into the back of his silver Navigator.

Tiberius smiled, watching Droopey get settled in the vehicle. He heard the soft yet persistent ring of his cell phone seconds before the unsettling vibrations began against his thigh. Checking the faceplate, he grinned at the sight of Roderick Jackson's name.

"Well, well. Haven't heard from you since the party!"

Roderick grinned at the sound of his friend's voice. "As a doctor you should understand being swamped beneath a crap-load of work."

Tiberius ordered Droopey to stay where she was by pointing a finger in her direction. "Say no more, man. We should try getting together soon though."

"No doubt. There was something I wanted to discuss with you anyway. No reason why we can't do it over drinks."

"Well give me a hint, man. Everything all right with Kiva?" Tiberius asked, referring to Rod's longtime girlfriend.

"Yeah, yeah, she's great. This is a real-estate question."

"Ah! My *other* job."

Again, Rod chuckled. "Right. I'm in the middle of wrapping up a conference now, so how about we get together to discuss it, have a few drinks while we're at it."

"Sounds good." Tiberius settled in behind the wheel as he and Roderick discussed particulars.

"Well, that's all I have," Capri said when they'd returned to Roderick's office later that afternoon to conclude the meeting. She stood and extended her hand toward Avery. "It was good to meet you. I'm looking forward to working together." She said, giving him her dazzling one-dimpled smile.

"Same here," Avery said, watching Capri nod in Rod's direction before she strolled out of the office. His eyes set on her full bottom pressed against the very flattering cut of the dress she wore.

Rod's laughter was close to the surface as he watched the helpless look on his friend's face. "Forget it, man," he called.

Avery's gaze was focused on the door as though he were still watching the provocative frame that had just exited the room. "Is she married?"

"No," Rod answered. "But forget it anyway. You'll never get anywhere with her."

"I get somewhere with every woman, my man," he bragged before slanting Rod a wink and leaving the office.

He caught up to Capri just as she turned into her office at the end of the long photo-lined corridor.

She had just taken a seat behind her desk when the knock sounded on her door. She was silent, watching as Avery peeked inside.

"Problem, Avery?"

"Just a question."

"Shoot." Capri leaned back and waited.

Avery was stealing a glimpse of the office, taking in the impressive portraits and photos decorating the walls and shelving.

"It may be a good idea to get together for drinks, you know? Get to know each other a bit better before we start the campaign," he suggested, while taking a closer look at the awards on the shelves near her desk.

"Get to know each other?"

Avery perched on the edge of the desk. "Yeah…ease the tension most people have between them when they first meet."

"Hmm…" Capri stood then and perched on the end of the desk opposite of Avery. "The only thing I need to know is your face and I'm afraid I can do that just fine without the aid of drinks."

"Ouch." Avery winced. "Not very smooth with that approach, am I?"

"I'm sure it'll be very successful on whomever you try it on next. Look, we're not gonna have any problems here, are we, Avery?"

He raised his hands defensively. "Not a one."

"Good." Capri's perky demeanor returned and she moved back to her desk chair. "Close the door on your way out, will you?"

Avery watched her for a moment longer, then shook his head and left the office. He saw Rod on his way down the hall and shrugged to concede the man's point. Rod's laughter filled the corridor.

Chapter 2

"Tiberius, can you please talk to this man?" Marilyn Joffey begged, spreading her hands wide across the desk.

Tiberius laughed at the forty-something couple seated before him. His patient Marilyn Joffey and her husband Gary were expecting their first child in less than a month. Leaning back in his huge leather chair, Tiberius scratched his eyebrow. "Exactly what is it you want me to talk to him about?"

Marilyn rolled her piercing green eyes toward her husband. "This man is about to drive me crazy with worry."

Tiberius smiled and nodded. "Marilyn, in all fairness, he is about to have his first child."

"Thank you," Gary spoke up, slamming his fist into the palm of his hand.

"Bull," Marilyn protested. "Tiberius, you don't have to live with him." Pushing herself up further in her chair, she pointed. "Do you know that he wakes me up in the middle of the night just to ask if I'm all right?"

Tiberius's rich, deep chuckles filled the spacious cream-and-beige office. "Gary? You might be taking this a bit too far, man."

Marilyn nodded. "See? I told you, he's a nervous wreck."

Laughing loudly now, Tiberius stood and walked around the side of his desk. "Trust me, Gary, everything's gonna be fine." He tried to reassure Gary, patting the man's shoulder.

The three of them talked for a while longer, with Tiberius going over a few notes he'd made during the ultrasound. As Marilyn was having her first child at the age of forty-one, Tiberius intended to be as thorough as possible. Their discussion covered every precaution regardless of how minor. Still, there was the matter of Gary's nerves. Once Marilyn was satisfied by her husband's vow to work harder on not driving himself or, more importantly, her, crazy with his angst, the couple prepared to leave.

Tiberius was still speaking to the expecting parents about their next appointment when his assistant buzzed through.

"Yes, Pam?" Tiberius hurriedly answered his assistant's call.

"Dr. Evans, I have your friend Roderick Jackson on the phone. He says if it's not too much of a bother, he'd like to reschedule your lunch today, to around two o'clock?"

Tiberius quickly scanned the calendar on his desk and nodded. "That sounds good to me. Tell him I'm looking forward to it."

Slamming her freshly filled tea glass to the table, Pepper Gregory narrowed a penetrating gray stare toward her friend. "This is hard to believe," she whispered.

Capri didn't bother looking up from the large green salad before her. "Why?"

"Why?" Pepper repeated, tapping one manicured nail against the smooth brown column of her neck. "Girl, I just can't believe you're tired of Miami. Tired of it enough to move out."

Shrugging, Capri munched on a forkful of lettuce, tomatoes and cucumber. "I'm not tired of Miami, I just need a change in atmosphere."

"Honey, do you realize how much you have going for you here?" Pepper questioned, pushing a lock of her thick, curled hair behind her ear. "Not to mention your fabulous job and friends."

"Pepper, look, for the last time, I'm not leaving the city altogether. I just don't want to be here day in and day out." Capri sighed, tugging on the lapels of her coatdress.

"Why?" Pepper asked, still bewildered. What could be better than living in the heart of the fast-paced, gorgeous city?

"Well, aside from just wanting more room to breathe, I'm sick of the same lines, and same approaches from men," Capri confided, propping her forehead in her hand. "I mean, don't get me wrong. I'm not trying to act like I've got men lined up all the way to the Keys, but it gets…wearisome."

Pepper sighed and propped her elbows on the table. "I can understand that. Men can be wonderful and aggravating all in the same breath sometimes."

"You've hit it on the head there, my friend." Capri groaned, her lovely dark eyes narrowing to slits. "I can handle it at work, but I guess now I'm craving a bit more distance from the hustle and bustle of it after five, you know?"

"Mmm…"

Capri scratched the hair that curled at her temple. "Lately…I don't know, it's just been so much of the same conversations that always lead to the *same* thing."

A tiny smile pulled at Pepper's mouth, as she closed her arms and watched her best friend.

"I don't know…" Capri sighed, eyes lifting to the mahogany bar directly across from the table. Her midnight stare met the unwavering one of the man sitting there. The incredibly handsome giant was staring at her, his deep-set eyes sending the most unfamiliar of tingles up her spine.

Capri's words trailed away as she became almost entranced by the man's fixed and probing stare. She glanced at Pepper, who was giving her a curious look, and cleared her throat. "Like this guy," she said, glancing at the bar again, "I can almost play out our first conversation in my head."

Pepper toyed with the braided gold chain around her neck and gave a nonchalant look in the same direction. She glanced toward the bar and did a double take when she saw the huge man watching her friend.

Although he wasn't looking at her, Pepper felt her own body

temperature rise. She fanned her hand in front of her face. "Ooo-wee."

"Definitely," Capri agreed, unable to ignore the man's sex appeal.

Pepper pulled her eyes away and focused on her macaroni salad. "I wondered how long it would take," she said mischievously.

Capri's dark eyes snapped up to Pepper's face. "How long *what* would take?"

"Honey, it's obvious the, uh, celibate life is getting to you," she replied without looking up.

"Wrong."

Finally Pepper looked up. "Girl, when are you gonna stop pretending you aren't human? It's okay to admit to your urges."

Capri rolled her eyes and said matter-of-factly, "the only urge I have is to get married one day and give myself to the man I'll spend the rest of my life with."

Pepper slapped her palm against the side of her face and stared wide-eyed into space. "That's a beautiful dream." She sighed. "But what the hell do you do in the meantime?"

"Don't even try it, Pep, you know I date," Capri argued. "Lately that's even gotten to be too aggravating. The men I seem to attract only want to go out for sex."

"Honey, do you realize how old you sound? I'm not knocking what you're saying, but you can't let a few bad apples spoil your fun."

Capri toyed with a few curly tendrils that fell from her up-do. "You just think sex is everything, and it isn't."

Pepper's light, lilting laugh turned more than a few male heads. "Honey, sex isn't everything, but it is a *big* thing. In some cases a *very* big thing," she added, casting another look in the direction of the sexy giant at the bar.

"Nasty," Capri chastised, before she began to laugh helplessly.

"So, tell me this, are you just gonna keep turning men away until one jumps in front of you and just happens to have all the qualities you're looking for?"

Capri sucked in her breath and raised her hand. "All right, I know what you're trying to say and I'm not that naive."

"Hmph, I sure hope not."

Capri groaned and brought her hand down on the table. "Look, Pepper, let me just put it this way, I've got three older sisters, all married to incredible guys—guys they saved themselves for." She shrugged, grimacing a bit at the fact. "I guess I just figure…"

"It's the natural order of things?" Pepper guessed, appearing as though she regretted pushing her friend into speaking on what was clearly a difficult subject.

Capri nodded. "I've placed all my decisions for much of my adult life on that very manner of thinking." She clenched a fist. "It's not so easy to admit that things may be meant to turn out differently for me. Not having an idea about it is…terrifying for lack of a better word." She fixed Pepper with a pleading look. "Try to bear with me a little here, will you?"

Pepper raised both hands in a defensive gesture. "All right, I won't say another word about it."

"Thanks. Now can we change the subject? Let's talk about something else."

A devious glint sparkled in Pepper's gray eyes. "Forget you. I'd rather talk to the guy at the bar."

"Here's another gin, Dr. Evans."

Tiberius smiled and took the fresh drink from the bartender. "Thanks, Ernie."

"No problem," Ernie Carson said, grinning in appreciation of the sizable tip Tiberius handed him. "Oh, and your friend Roderick Jackson just got here, he's waiting at your table on the other side. The hostess will show you."

"Thanks again, man," Tiberius said, easing his huge, athletic form from the barstool. Before leaving, he cast another look across the room at the tiny beauty with the gorgeous body. With a quick shake of his head he ordered himself to forget the delights of pleasure and remember the frustration of misunderstandings.

"What's goin' on, man?" Rod greeted, smiling when he spotted Tiberius approaching the table.

Tiberius grinned, his deep-set eyes crinkling slightly at the corners. "Not a damn thing. Working, working and working."

The two friends hugged each other tightly before taking their seats at the table. For a while, the men simply stared at each other, until Tiberius laughed.

Rod laughed, as well, and shook his head. "Man, what the hell is wrong with you?"

"How long has it been since we've been sitting in a restaurant together, kid?" Tiberius asked, between chuckles.

"I know, right?" Rod asked, smoothing his hand over his close-cut hair. "Like you said, working, working and working."

"Mmm-hmm." Tiberius sighed, taking a sip of his gin. "So how's Kiva?"

A mischievous grin crossed Rod's face as his thoughts settled on his live-in lover Kiva Reynolds. "She's good. I'm inching toward asking her the big question."

Tiberius took the last swallow of his drink. "What question?" he asked absently.

Rod rolled his eyes. "Man, the *big* question. I'm gonna ask her to marry me."

Tiberius stared at Rod for a moment, before groaning. "Ah, Rod, man…are you sure?"

"Hell yeah, I'm sure. After four years I should be sure," Rod firmly replied, a deep furrow forming between his sleek brows. Sitting back in his chair, Rod regarded Tiberius with a suspicious glare. "What's up, man, I always thought you liked Kiva?"

Tiberius shook his head, holding his hand out across the table.

"Rod, don't get me wrong. I love Kiva. I hope it works out for y'all."

"Mmm-hmm. So what are *you* waiting on?" Rod's voice was cool, though the curiosity was apparent in his tone.

Tiberius's heavy dark brows drew close as he frowned at his friend. "What am I waiting on to get married? Nothing. Because I'm never doing it."

Rod laughed. "Whatever you say, man."

Tiberius didn't appreciate Rod's humor. "What's so funny?"

"Man, when you finally meet *the* woman, you'll be singing a different tune. I guarantee it," Rod predicted.

"I doubt it."

Rod was still laughing when the waitress came to the table to take their orders. Rod was barely able to control his chuckles as he placed his order. Tiberius, however, retained his cool, serious demeanor.

"Now, why does your friend seem to be in such a good mood and you don't?" the waitress asked when Tiberius gave her his order.

"Because he's a very sick man and doesn't know it."

"Hey!" a wounded Rod cried.

The waitress laughed, unable to pull her brown eyes away from Tiberius's face. "Well, I hope your day will improve."

Tiberius rolled his eyes away from Rod to look into the waitress's lovely face. "Thanks. I'm pretty sure it'll shape up from here on out." He told her, his voice soft and deep.

The waitress's sparkling smile only became brighter and she bowed her head. "Glad I could help."

Tiberius leaned back in his chair and propped his index finger alongside his temple. "I'm glad you could, too."

Meanwhile, Rod was shaking his head at Tiberius's awesome talent for flirting. When the waitress left with their orders, Rod continued to stare at his friend.

"What?" Tiberius asked, shifting his gaze toward Rod.

"Nothing." Rod sighed, leaning back in his own chair. "So, how's your love life going?"

The look in Tiberius's light-brown eyes became devious. "It's not." His expression became deeply serious for the first time since he'd met his friend at the table.

"Forgive me, I should have asked about your sex life."

Grinning at the dig, Tiberius shrugged. "My answer would be the same."

"What's this? Casanova dissatisfied?"

"Just taking a break from all the crap."

Rod chuckled and took a sip from his water glass. "Sometimes it can be worth it. When you fall in love you'll see what I mean."

A horrified look crossed Tiberius's handsome face. "Man, please don't put that on me."

Rod shook his head and gave Tiberius a confused look. "All right, what's goin' on with you? You're more cynical than usual."

Tiberius shrugged his shoulders. "You know, Rod, all the women I know, and I don't think I'll ever figure them out."

"Which one's got you in an uproar now?" Rod asked, preparing himself for one of the colorful stories Tiberius always had to tell about his long list of female friends.

Tiberius fidgeted with the silverware peeking from the edge of his napkin. "It's not one woman, actually, just women in general. From the crazy and scary to the terrific and nurturing," he said, thinking of his patient, Marilyn Joffey. "Guess I can't help thinking how great it'd be to find *the* one without all the craziness that tends to go along with it."

Rod kept his gaze on the table. "And you're sure this has nothing to do with you being ready to fall in love and take the step?"

"Positive," Tiberius assured his friend, though his voice had lost a bit of its edge. "With that house sitting empty, I guess maybe the entire commitment thing's been on my mind more lately. That cottage was my grandmother's favorite, you know?" He slanted Rod a quick smile and then shook his head. "I always asked her why she didn't just get rid of the headache of those houses and sell them. She could've made a killing. She told me there was something solid about a house, how the folks inside had plans for longevity. She loved renting to couples."

The waitress returned with fresh drinks. She was far less talkative than before, obviously sensing a more serious mood had fallen over her two patrons.

Rod thanked her with a smile and a brief nod. He knew better than anyone how close Tiberius had been to his late grandmother Janice Evans. It was one reason why he'd maintained the houses instead of selling them as he'd been advised. She had been more of a parent to Tiberius than his own had been.

Hoping to pull his friend out of the doldrums that overshadowed Tiberius whenever he thought of Janice, Rod knocked his fist to the table and grinned. "Funny you should mention the cottage. I might be able to help you out with that."

"How's that?"

"Well, it's no couple, but I've got a friend who's thinking of moving out of the city and I told her I knew somebody who rented houses and I'd check it out for her."

Tiberius nodded and sent Rod a knowing smirk. "I don't see any problem with it, but how high-strung is she?"

"Hmph, the woman works too hard to be high-strung," Rod noted.

Tiberius stroked the smooth skin of his jaw. "What does she do?"

"She works with me at Grant and Shields."

"She's a photographer?"

"Uh-huh. She works for a lot of uh, women's magazines. The ones that feature…nude art, if you get my meaning."

Tiberius raised his brows. By the look on his face it was clear that he was very impressed. He reached into his jacket pocket and retrieved a card from his wallet. "Here's my lawyer's card. Tell your friend to give him a call."

Chapter 3

Capri's cool, airy condominium was barely recognizable with all the boxes cluttering the floors. The elegant furniture was hidden beneath clothes, boxes and art. The entire place looked as though it had been hit by a tornado.

After Rod had told her about the house being available, Capri had wasted no time in calling the lawyer and getting the paperwork started. She had even begun the necessary steps to lease her condo. In preparation for the Bare Minimum photo campaign and going through the motions to prepare for the move from the condo, eight weeks had passed rather quickly. Between meetings with her photography crew and meetings with potential lessees for the condo, she'd had to cancel out on seeing the cottage four times already.

Still, she didn't want to risk missing out on acquiring the place. Though she realized she hadn't seen the house before committing to it, Capri wasn't worried. She already knew a lot about the Seaside Trace area of Miami where the house was located and couldn't wait to move.

Capri was in the master bedroom and almost didn't hear the phone ringing in the living room. She had already unplugged all the phones in the other rooms, leaving only one operable. Of course, when she made it to the cluttered room, she had to take a few minutes to locate where the ringing was coming from. Shuffling through a heap of T-shirts and jeans on the sofa, she found the small slender cordless.

"Hello?" she quickly answered.

Tiberius smiled and took a moment to reply to the woman's breathless greeting. "May I speak with Capri Timmons?"

The deep, smooth voice on the other end brought Capri up short. "This is Capri," she replied, very softly.

"Ms. Timmons, this is Tiberius Evans. I believe you'll be renting my house?"

"Yes, yes," Capri answered, smiling brightly as she flopped down on the cluttered sofa. "Listen, thanks so much for letting me rent the place."

Again, Tiberius smiled. "No problem. I'm just glad I had one available. There is one problem, though."

"Oh no, what?"

"Well, I just don't feel right about renting you a house you haven't seen yet."

Capri expressed the breath she'd been holding and gave a nervous laugh. "I'm sorry I haven't been able to keep those appointments, things have been crazy on my end."

"Well, I'd really like you to see it," Tiberius replied, the words sounding firm.

Running her fingers through her soft curls, Capri leaned back against the sofa. "So would I." She sighed, silently cursing herself for not having already done so. "I've been a little anxious to get out of the city."

Tiberius's warm, deep chuckle vibrated through the phone line. "I can understand that, but I'd just feel a lot better if you saw it first. Are you free to come out and today and take a look at it?"

"I get the feeling you won't take no for an answer?" Capri asked, finding his determination appealing.

"Only if you make me."

The easy response sent something swirling in her chest, but it was gone before she could pinpoint what it was. At any rate, going out to see her new home as quickly as possible had been on her mind. Capri had figured she'd have to wait since her schedule was always so hectic. Today, however, would be perfect since she'd already spent her assigned half day at the studio. Sighing, she glanced at her watch before slapping her hand against the arm of the sofa. "All right, what time?"

It didn't take Capri very long to locate her soon-to-be new neighborhood. She'd been through the lovely, quiet area several times and always saw homes that made her eyes widen. One of her favorite pastimes had been to hop in her car and take a drive through a beautiful development.

Capri was over an hour early for her meeting with Tiberius. He'd already told her he'd be home well into the afternoon, barring any emergencies at the hospital. She decided it couldn't hurt to head out early in case she had trouble finding the house.

Of course, every home in the neighborhood was lovely and sat on an impressive landscape. However, when Capri finally parked her chocolate Pathfinder, she was completely taken away by the house she stood in front of.

"This is it," she breathed, taking small steps up the brick driveway that curved before the house like a horseshoe. The area of lawn growing inside the curve of the driveway was perfectly manicured and a healthy green color. The house itself looked as if it could shelter a small army. The massive brick structure sat amidst several gigantic palm trees and Capri was sure it could've been selected for a *Beautiful Homes* cover.

The double front door of the house was a high structure with a pair of marble columns on either side. There were bay windows on each side of the door as well as equally large windows showing along the upper level of the house. Spotlights on the roof at every corner provided security, while at the same time giving the house a modern appearance.

The rear of the house was shielded from view by a tall, wooden fence. Capri stared at the structure for a moment, before turning toward the front of the house again. Taking a deep breath she smoothed nonexistent wrinkles from her clothing. The petal-pink,

V-neck T-shirt dress she wore reached her midthigh. Her only jewelry was two pairs of tiny diamond studs in her double pierced ears and a diamond anklet.

Capri knocked on the door several times. When there was no answer, she stood on the toes of her white tennis shoes and peeked through the tiny stained-glass windows on either side of the doors. Unfortunately, it was impossible to see anything through them.

"Well, I *am* early," Capri whispered, glancing at her watch. She had decided to wait awhile in her truck, when she heard a bass tone drifting from the back of the house.

Slowly, Capri followed the sound, pausing to listen for a moment. She could clearly detect the music coloring the air. She pushed the tall, wooden gate of the fence open and entered. Her dark eyes widened in surprise and her mouth fell open at the sight before her.

Tiberius had his back turned, while he concentrated on washing his truck. He was dressed in a pair of denim shorts that sagged below his waist and stopped just below his knees. His toned, muscular upper body was bare and glistened with sweat beneath the late-afternoon sun.

Though Tiberius was unaware that someone had just entered his backyard, Droopey was on the case. The collie saw the tiny woman standing just inside the gate and began to bark. She jumped up from her position on the large deck and ran across the yard.

Capri saw the dog heading for her, but wasn't afraid. She knelt to the ground and prayed the animal was friendly. Her prayer was answered. Droopey sniffed the unfamiliar body for a moment and found nothing to dislike. In seconds, Droopey was licking Capri's hands and neck.

From the corner of his eye, Tiberius saw his dog jump off the deck and looked in the direction she was heading. For a moment, he was utterly speechless. Bracing one hand against the hood of his truck, his light-brown eyes narrowed. He watched the petite, vaguely familiar lady petting his dog. Then, after wiping the soap from his hands, he decided to investigate.

Capri was giggling helplessly from the friendly dog's wet kisses. She stopped petting Droopey and stood when she saw a pair of heavily muscled male legs before her. When she looked into the man's incredibly handsome face, her eyes narrowed. The same was true for Tiberius as his mouth dropped open and the beginnings of a smile began to form.

"You."

"You."

Each took a moment to view up close what had only been seen from a distance. Capri was the first to pull herself out of the trance. Extending her hand, she smiled.

"Dr. Tiberius Evans?"

Tibe nodded. "Capri Timmons?"

"Mmm-hmm…" Capri confirmed, unable to keep her eyes from sliding across Tiberius' wide chest.

Tiberius noticed the direction of her gaze and glanced down. "Sorry for not being dressed. I, um…" He trailed away, looking at his watch.

In an innocent manner, Capri laid her hands across Tiberius's wrist. "No you're fine, I'm the one who screwed up the time. Actually I wanted to come out a little early in case I got lost."

Tiberius just stared at Capri, not even realizing how affected he was by her touch, or that he was staring for that matter. Of course, Capri didn't mind, since she'd been doing the same thing.

"Would you like to come inside while I change into something more appropriate?"

Capri nodded and gave him a quick smile. Tiberius waved his hand before them. His eyes never strayed as she walked past him. Once again, his gaze narrowed while he took time to admire her shapely form.

"You all right?" Tiberius asked, when he heard her tiny gasp.

Capri pushed back a curly lock of hair that had fallen from her high ponytail and nodded. "Your house is even more beautiful from the inside."

Tiberius smiled at the compliment and took a moment to look around the bright sitting room they'd entered through the side door. The room was really a mass of sofas and armchairs situated around magazine-filled glass coffee tables. Still, it was extremely lovely.

Capri walked around the room gazing at the high ceiling. The furniture was white with gold trim. It all had her speechless.

Tiberius shook his head as though he were clearing his mind. He'd had countless women in his home, many times. Still, he'd never found himself just staring. Well, staring yes, but never in the helpless manner he was just now.

Clearing his throat, it only took a few steps to bring him next to Capri. "Do you need me to get you anything?" He politely asked, laying one hand against her waist.

Unaccustomed to the tingles running through her body, Capri took a moment to answer. Although she wasn't some boy crazy high-school girl, she couldn't help the path her eyes took. They slid from the top of his curly, black hair, over his incredibly handsome face and then his tall, powerful frame.

"I'm fine." She finally answered in a small voice.

"You just make yourself comfortable then, and I'm going to change."

Capri watched his huge, lithe body race up the stairway and shook her head. Taking advantage of the time alone, she took her own personal tour of the house. Of all the times she'd driven through the neighborhood, this was her first opportunity to see the inside of one of the houses. Surprisingly, it met with every one of her expectations. The stately appearance of the mansion on the outside had had her speechless earlier. Now, it was the cozy, lived-in yet cool elegance of the home's interior that held her entranced.

While she was browsing, Capri had wandered into one of the

many hallways. This one in particular was filled with gorgeous paintings. Each of the large pictures seemed to begin an image that was completed on the next canvas. She'd been studying one of them and stepped back to get a better look, when she bumped against a warm, hard surface.

Tiberius brought his hands up around Capri's upper arms and steadied her. He held her against him, then let go so quickly that the embrace might have been imagined.

"This is very nice, Dr. Evans." Capri sighed, trying to begin conversation and hoping she didn't sound as nervous as she felt.

Tiberius's sexy mouth tilted upwards in a knowing smile. He scratched one of his heavy black brows and walked away from Capri. "Are you ready to see your own place?" he called over his shoulder.

"Yes," she breathed, grateful for the chance to break the electricity in the room.

With Droopey following along, Tiberius took Capri to the house next door. It had one huge, curving brick step leading to a lovely brick house. There were huge windows with yellow roses at the sills. Capri could see that there was a spacious patio on the rear overlooking the backyard filled with shady palms.

"Ooh, Lewey's gonna love that big yard."

Tiberius grinned as he unlocked the door. "Is that your little dog?"

"Yeah, that's my baby." Unease tinged her gaze then. "I hope it's okay to have him out here?"

Tiberius was already waving his hand. "Droopey'll be happy for the company," he said, pushing the door open and then standing back to let Capri enter.

"Oh my God," she whispered.

"Something wrong?" he asked, hoping the year-old remodeling job met with her approval.

Capri looked at Tiberius as though he had two heads. "It's perfect! Lord, look at all this space! I can't believe how big it is!"

"Yeah, it tends to look real small from the outside," Tiberius called, though he was sure Capri didn't hear him. She was racing through every room ooohing and aaaahing. Crossing his arms over his chest, Tiberius leaned against the front doorjamb and watched her.

"So I take it you like it?" he asked, when she finally returned to the living room.

Capri clasped her hands together and closed her eyes. "I can't wait to move in, Dr. Evans, I'm so glad you asked me to come see it today."

Tiberius sighed and pulled one hand through his thick hair. "You're welcome, but can you please start calling me by my first name? I don't mind."

"I certainly will. And you can call me Capri."

"I was planning on it."

Capri ordered herself not to become affected by the firm, deep quality of Tiberius's voice. "Now I'm even more excited about leaving my condo," she said, trying once more to spark conversation.

Tiberius pushed his hands deep into the pockets of his nylon sweatpants. "So what's the problem with the city?"

"Being hit on twenty times a night has made it stifling," Capri blurted.

Tiberius's loud rolling laughter filled the living room and Capri closed her eyes in regret.

"Well, Capri, in defense of my fellow man I'd have to admit that I understand their reasons."

The tortured tone of Tiberius's voice brought a smile to Capri's face. She realized that normally she would've been aggravated, but surprisingly she wasn't. Nodding, she acknowledged what sounded more like a compliment than a line.

"So, if you're serious about the house I can give you the key right now," Tiberius finally told her, breaking into the silence that had fallen over the room.

Excitement brightened Capri's small, lovely face. She jumped from the sofa and practically snatched the house key from his hand. "Tiberius, thanks so much, you won't regret this."

"No, I don't think I will."

Capri cleared her throat. Her nerves switched to overdrive in response to the intense look in Tiberius's gorgeous light-brown eyes. "I have a lot to do, so I'd better go on and leave."

Tiberius pulled the door shut behind them and watched Capri who was already headed across the lawn. Drawing his lower lip between his teeth, he debated.

"Capri?"

"Yeah?"

"I was going to throw a steak on the grill for dinner. I wouldn't mind fixing two."

A faint voice in the back of Capri's mind told her she should refuse. This man was far too sexy and she was already far too attracted to keep a clear head. *Girl when are you gonna stop pretending you aren't human…admit to your urges.* This time, it was Pepper's firm voice that broke into Capri's thoughts. Shrugging, she tapped her fingers against the neckline of her dress and headed back toward Tiberius. It wouldn't hurt just to have dinner with the man, she decided.

"As nice as it is out here, I can't just sit around while you do all the cooking."

Tiberius leaned against the large, brick kitchen island and watched Capri. "Most women would take advantage of this."

Capri propped one hand on her hip. "I'm not most women."

"No, you aren't." Tiberius couldn't resist sliding his gaze across her tiny, sensual form.

"Good, then I insist on helping."

Tiberius scratched his head and strode across the kitchen to the colossal refrigerator in the far corner. "Let's see...all right, you can fix the salad."

"No problem," Capri said, slapping her hands together.

The two of them spent the next twenty minutes in the large, well-equipped kitchen. The walls and the island in the center of the room were brick. The floor was burgundy tile and all the appliances were cream-colored. An easy mood had settled over the kitchen. The only sounds were the crunching of vegetables and herbs or the clattering of utensils.

Capri found everything she needed to prepare a delicious salad. She chopped several types of vegetables and even gathered the necessary ingredients to prepare a creamy Italian dressing.

Meanwhile, Tiberius tenderized and seasoned two beautifully cut steaks, prepared potatoes for the grill, and selected a wine.

Of course, their attentions weren't focused solely on the food. Many times, they were distracted by each other's bodies. Capri was very taken by Tiberius's size. Her dark eyes repeatedly trailed over his broad shoulders, chest and back beneath his gray sweatshirt. What held her fascination most were his hands. One hand could easily cover both of hers.

Tiberius also found his eyes wandering several times. Though Capri had a very slim frame, her breasts were quite ample. The round globes looked as though they belonged on someone much larger. While her short tennis dress wasn't skin-tight, Tiberius could tell that she had a very small waistline and hips, but her derriere was surprisingly full. A low groan came from his chest as he prayed for strength to keep things light and platonic.

Capri glanced up at Tiberius and their gazes held. "So, um, what type of doctor are you?"

"An obstetrician."

"Really?"

"You sound surprised."

"Well, you just don't look like, I mean…"

Tiberius chuckled and raised one hand. "Don't worry about it. A lot of people are surprised when I tell them. I guess they think I look like a brain surgeon or something."

"That's more like it," Capri nodded, though she couldn't help but look at his hands again. They were large and strong, perfect for guiding a baby into a new world. "So do you mind me asking why you settled on being an obstetrician?" she asked lightly while chopping a cucumber.

Tiberius cleared his throat over the swell of emotion suddenly lodged there. Of course, the true tug toward obstetrics was rooted in a childhood spent trying to please two demanding yet absentee parents. Choosing not to mar the makings of a nice evening with such a story, he shrugged and gave her his standby reason.

"Dr. Heathcliff Huxtable," he announced with pride and a fair amount of humor in his voice.

Capri dissolved into laughter.

"What?" Tiberius pretended to be confused. "I never missed an episode of *The Cosby Show*."

Still laughing, Capri shook her head and glanced down at her appetizing salad before carrying it over to the refrigerator. "Well, I'm all done with this. Can I help you with anything else?"

"Out," Tiberius ordered, pointing in the direction of the deck.

Capri was lounging on the deck when Tiberius came to put the steaks on the grill. Smiling to herself, she thought about how out of character all this was for her. Having dinner at the home of a man she barely knew, relaxing on his gorgeous comfortable patio. No, this wasn't the Capri Timmons she knew.

Tiberius looked over at Capri lying back on one of the cushiony chaise lounges. Damn, she was such a lovely thing. She was shorter and smaller than what he was used to but still lovely. He'd already decided not to become romantically involved with his next tenant if it were a woman. Unfortunately, he hadn't counted on Capri striking him the way she had. Keeping his distance would be tougher than he thought.

The cool, relaxing sounds of a vintage R&B single drifted out to the deck and Capri smiled. "Is that the radio?"

"Close, it's a CD," Tiberius informed her, placing two potatoes wrapped in foil on the grill.

"You have the *Love Jones* soundtrack?" Capri asked, raising her head.

"Yeah, is that okay?"

"No, it's perfect. I haven't heard it in the longest time."

"Did you ever see the movie?"

Capri sighed and toyed with one of her curls. "It's been a while. I actually can't recall the last time I've taken time to enjoy any of the movies in my collection."

"Damn, you work that hard?"

"I work that hard."

Tiberius set the platter in his hand at the side of the grill and walked over to Capri. Taking a seat on her lounge, he propped his cheek on his fist. "Rod told me what you do."

"I bet he did. What'd he say? That I photograph men in the nude?"

Tiberius chuckled. "No, but I got the point."

Capri shrugged and threw her arms across the back of the lounge behind her head. "Well, I'm good at it and it pays the bills."

"I hear that."

"And?" Capri asked, seeing the questioning look in his light-brown eyes.

"And what?"

"And don't you have something more to ask me. Most people are full of questions when they find out what I do."

Tiberius nodded and braced his fingers together. "Well, it's hard to believe you work around so many men and one of them hasn't snatched you up."

"You have to know how to separate work from play."

"So you don't date the men you meet on the job?"

"I prefer not to."

Tiberius was obviously finding everything hard to believe and he began to chuckle. Capri smiled as well, loving the dimples in his cheeks. "What's so funny?"

"I was just wondering what's wrong with the guys you live around?"

"You'd know if you could hear some of those tired lines they use. It's so obvious what they want and it'd probably be easier to skip the lines and just be up front about it."

"And if they were up front about it, would you still be interested?"

"Probably not." Capri laughed at the irony of it all.

Tiberius let his eyes drift over Capri's bare arms and legs. "I don't think leaving Miami will allow you to completely avoid men who don't have that on their minds."

Capri cleared her throat and pulled her legs beneath her. "Well, when they're so obvious about it all I want is to laugh in their faces."

Tiberius stood up from the lounge. "Give 'em a break. Most of us lose our minds in the presence of a woman who looks like you," he replied softly, before walking away.

Chapter 4

Capri stretched her arms high above her head and snuggled deeper into the soft mattress. A satisfied smile pulled at her mouth as she moaned. It was late the next morning and she'd already overslept. Being caught up in the midst of a sensual dream starring Dr. Tiberius Evans was making it difficult to wake up.

Finally the phone began to ring, succeeding in tugging Capri from her slumber. "Mmm… Hello?"

The lazy, satisfied tone of Capri's voice surprised Pepper, who was on the other end. Since she usually had one thing on her mind, Pepper immediately assumed her best friend was up to something naughty. "Girl, what are you doing?" she quickly asked in a hushed tone.

Capri pushed one hand through her curly locks and sighed. "Pepper. Well…I was having a very good dream."

Pepper gave a short laugh and rolled her eyes to the ceiling. "Well, if it works for you. So what's on your schedule for today?"

"Rod gave me the day off to move so…"

"Wait a minute. You're leaving today?"

"Mmm-hmm, the movers should be here in a couple of hours."

"Damn, you ain't wasting time haulin' ass out of there, are you?"

"Hell no, and I can't afford to. That house won't be free for long."

"Didn't you say he rents places all around his home?" Pepper asked, waiting until she heard Capri's response before continuing. "Doesn't he have any others?"

"I asked about that." Capri rolled to her back and drew a hand through her hair again. "He said the cottage had been hardest to occupy for any lengthy stretch of time. All the other tenants are couples with and without kids. People looking to put down roots, you know? For some reason, he hasn't had a lot of success with the place closest to his own home."

Pepper's arched brows raised another notch. "So do you think *you'll* be happy there?"

"After seeing it, I honestly couldn't imagine myself being *unhappy* there."

Pepper could hear the excitement fringing Capri's words and it was contagious. "So could you use some more help?"

Capri laughed. "What time can you be here?"

Tiberius had been awake for some time, but had yet to pull himself out of bed. He stared at the ceiling, watching the sun trying to invade the room from over the tops of the long, dark-blue drapes. As he lay there, stroking his muscled abdomen partially hidden beneath the sheet, he thought about his new tenant.

By now, he'd gotten used to the fact that Capri was going to be no less than a hundred feet from him. Still, he debated whether to pursue her. Of course, he knew it would inevitably lead to trouble, but he also knew that fact had never stopped him before. He couldn't remember the last time he'd been alone with a beautiful woman in his home and not made love to her. It was refreshing, but Tiberius knew he had Capri to thank for that. She was so laid-back and easy to talk to. He'd never realized how nice a conversation with a woman could be without all the sexual innuendo that almost always came into play.

A devious smirk added a sinister element to his honey-toned features. He still couldn't get over how lovely she was, how provocative. He had to admit that Capri had something different. Whether he was simply infatuated or that something different was really genuine, he didn't know. She was like a cross between innocent little girl and seductive temptress. The mixture was very intoxicating.

Tiberius closed his eyes and produced a vivid picture of Capri Timmons in his mind. It was surprising that a woman like that didn't have a man in her life. Thinking about her had surely awakened his desire. Tiberius groaned when his gaze settled to the crisp sheet lying low across his hips. It had risen into the tell-tale tent shape. Dragging himself out of bed, he decided it was time for a cold shower.

"Oh, baby, don't be that way!"

"Cutie, come on over here and lemme talk to ya!"

Pepper laughed and waved at the men calling to her. She'd just arrived at Capri's building and assumed all the huge, burly men lifting furniture were movers. Of course, they couldn't resist shouting compliments or stopping to watch her walk by.

Pepper, however, never minded things like that. She just laughed, tossed her thick hair over her shoulder and sauntered away to Capri's place.

"Hey, girl, what's up?" she called to Capri when she found her in the kitchen.

"Morning. You ready to work?" Capri asked, sounding very chipper.

"Where do I start?"

"Well…let's see." Capri sighed, looking around the cluttered kitchen. "I'm almost through wrapping the glasses, so next are the dishes and I'll be done."

"Damn, Cappy." Pepper sighed, leaning against the counter. "I can't believe all this happened so fast."

"I know, I never thought when I moved out of here I'd ever be moving into a house."

"So what's your new landlord like?"

A mischievous smirk appeared on Capri's face. "Actually, you already met him."

"'Scuse me?"

Capri cleared her throat and packed the last of the glasses away in a box. "Dr. Tiberius Evans is the same guy we saw in the restaurant, sitting at the bar. I told you I figured I had him pegged."

Pepper frowned, as she took a moment to remember the day of that particular lunch date. Soon though, realization dawned and her eyes widened. "Nooo? Cap, you're just lyin' to me, right?"

"Wrong."

"Damn, you are the luckiest person I know."

"Then you don't know very many people."

Pepper shook her head as she began to wrap the plates. "I can't believe that fine-ass man is your landlord. I guess you'll be wanting to deliver your rent checks in person."

"Whatever, Pepper." Capri sighed, amused by her friend's one-track mind.

"Ah, come on, don't tell me you won't take a special trip to his office once a month for one reason or another?"

"I won't have to, since he lives right next door."

Pepper set the plate down. "Next door? To you?"

"Mmm-hmm."

"Damn."

"We had dinner at his house, too," Capri revealed, finding much enjoyment in shocking Pepper.

"Wait a minute. The man lives right next door and you already had dinner together?"

"That's right."

Pepper glared across the room waiting for more information. "And?" she finally barked.

"And what?" Capri absently replied, concentrating on wrapping a huge casserole dish. Glancing up at Pepper, she saw the knowing look on her face. "Nothing happened, Pep."

"The hell it didn't. Girl, you've never gone to a man's house for dinner unless there were at least two other people there, too."

"Well, there weren't."

"And you did it anyway, hmph. Damn, he must be somethin'."

"It was only dinner."

Pepper pushed her hands into the side pockets of her black cotton bellbottoms and fixed Capri with a knowing stare. "This time it was only dinner, but next time…"

Capri closed her eyes and regretted she'd even mentioned Tiberius. "Pepper you're getting excited for nothing. There's nothing to this."

"Cappy, I've seen this man."

"So have I. Twice. And I get the feeling that the good doctor is used to getting women in bed anytime he wants to. I'm trying to avoid men like that. One of the reasons I'm moving, remember?"

"Ha! Good luck Capri. If you can stay away from a man like that, you must have an iron will."

Kiva Reynolds threw back her long, micro-thin braids and pushed herself up in bed. Pulling the crisp linen sheets around either side of her hips, she gazed down at the handsome dark man beneath her and smiled.

Rod returned his girlfriend's knowing smile and trailed his hands across her flawless chocolate skin. His slanting black stare followed the path of his hands. They grazed across Kiva's strong thighs, her flat stomach, round breasts and finally to her lovely face. The beauty sitting astride him awakened his desire immediately.

Kiva gasped and her clear deep-brown eyes widened when she felt Rod harden again inside of her. "I can't believe you're ready again."

"You know how I do," Rod seductively replied, closing his eyes in satisfaction.

Kiva's head fell back and she began to move her hips back and forth. Deep moans and loud cries soon filled the elegantly furnished room. Sex between them had always been hot and furious. Still, it was the love and commitment they had for one another that made it all sizzle. They enjoyed each other enthusiastically, until Kiva fell across Rod's chest and begged for mercy.

"Mmm… Stay home today, baby," she whispered into his neck.

Rod smiled and caressed Kiva's back and buttocks. "I wish I could, believe me. But there's a meeting at the agency I have to be in on."

"Nooo…" she groaned, inching over to her side of the bed. "Can't Capri handle it?"

"She could, but I gave her the day off so she could move."

"Move?" Kiva parroted, sitting up. "So she really did it, I haven't talked to her about it in weeks."

Rod yawned as he spoke. "Damn right she did it. Got a house and everything."

"Oh, well, that's great. Her own house. I'm proud of her."

"Yeah, Tiberius had a vacancy in one of the places he rents out, so I arranged for Cappy to get it." Rod coolly revealed, pleased with himself.

Kiva, however, wasn't quite as pleased. "Tiberius…are you sure that's a good idea?"

"Excuse me?"

"Well, you know, having her living so close to Tiberius. You think it'll go smoothly?"

Rod frowned and pushed himself up on his elbows. "Hell yeah, I think it'll go smoothly. What's wrong with you?"

Kiva held out her hands defensively. "Look, you know I adore

Tiberius. But you also know how, um…sexually focused he is and…"

"It's strictly business, Kiva."

Kiva's expression was one of total disbelief. "Has he met Capri yet?"

Rod rolled his eyes toward the ceiling fan and sighed. "I know what you're saying."

"I hope so."

Tiberius leaned against the hood of his truck and glanced over his calendar. Standing there with his head tilted and his light-brown eyes narrowed in concentration, he portrayed a completely alluring picture.

Noise from next door attracted his attention and he saw the moving vans. Tiberius shook his head at how crazy things seemed. Instead of there being over a year since the last tenant it seemed more like a week between someone leaving and someone new arriving.

One of Tiberius's deep dimples appeared as a cunning smirk crossed his full lips. He saw Capri standing behind her Pathfinder, pulling a box from the rear. Pushing his hands into the deep pockets of his lightweight beige trousers, he watched her for a while. His gaze lowered from the top of her head to slide over her green halter top and the worn fitted jeans that hung low over her hips. Tiberius threw his BlackBerry into the Navigator and headed over.

Capri had praised her luck when she'd found a box large enough to pack all her photo equipment together. Now, she cursed it, since she was finding the box next to impossible to lift. Still, she didn't trust the movers to use infinite care with her most prized possessions.

"Can I help you with that?"

Capri shook her head when she heard the deep voice behind her. "That's okay I almost have it," she answered politely. In the next instant she was gasping at the feel of a hand on her hip. Forgetting the box, Capri whipped her head around.

"You sure?" Tiberius asked, his brown eyes twinkling at her expression.

"Tiberius," Capri sighed, giving a breathless laugh. "I just want you to know you came this close to a painful mishap," she informed him, placing her index finger over her thumb.

"Ouch. It's been one of those days, huh?"

"Nah, the movers are perfect gentlemen."

Tiberius threw his head back and laughed, Capri took a moment to let her eyes glide over his wide chest and shoulders, encased beneath a collarless beige suit coat.

"So where are you off to looking so smooth?" Capri teased, but the compliment was sincere.

"Well thanks," Tiberius replied, smiling and very pleased by her words. "I'm on my way to work."

"Hmph."

"What?"

Capri shrugged. "Nothing. You just talk about it like it's a regular job."

Tiberius, who still had his hand resting against Capri's hip, patted her there absently. "Oh, I know it's not, believe me. I take what I do very seriously."

"I don't doubt that for a minute," Capri softly replied, her large dark eyes roaming helplessly over his face.

All attempts at conversation left them, and an awkward silence settled between them.

"Cap!"

A relieved smile brightened Capri's face when she heard Pepper yelling. Turning, she waved and beckoned her best friend to join her and Tiberius.

"What's wrong?" Capri asked as soon as Pepper approached the truck.

"Nothing, I just didn't know where you were," Pepper explained absently, her gray stare already focused on Tiberius.

Capri shook her head at her friend's interest. "Pepper, this is my landlord and next-door neighbor Tiberius Evans. Tiberius, this is Priscilla Gregory, my best friend."

After the introductions, Tiberius and Pepper shook hands. Pepper's face held the same expression of a loyal fan meeting favorite celebrity.

"Nice to meet you, Priscilla," Tiberius greeted Pepper.

"Um…thank you, thank you, but please call me Pepper and let me just say you have a fantastic home. All of them."

"Thanks Pepper, just make sure your girl doesn't burn this one down." Tiberius teased, making them laugh.

"Ha! You're talkin' to the wrong person," Capri bellowed.

Tiberius shook his head and sighed at the two beautiful women who stood beside him. "Well, y'all just watch each other. Pepper, it was good meeting you. Capri, I'll see you later."

Capri smiled and nodded in Tiberius's direction, her eyes following him across the lawn. After a moment, she turned her attention back to the large box in her trunk. Feeling Pepper's knowing gaze on her, she slammed her hand against the box. "What, Pep?"

"Did I say he was fine? Girl, he is beyond that."

Capri rolled her eyes and concentrated on pulling the box from the trunk. "You really need to get over this hang-up you have about looks. Help me with this, why don't you?"

Pepper pretended to be surprised. "Why does it have to be a hang-up? I just happen to like attractive men."

"You just happen to be obsessed with attractive men."

"Whatever." Pepper sighed, raising her hand. "I was only tryin' to say the man was gorgeous, sexy and very nice and that's something even you can't deny," she stated, shooting Capri an angry glare before taking the opposite end of the large box of photo equipment.

Several hours later, with the help of the movers and Pepper, Capri had settled into her new home. The spacious interior of the place had allowed Capri to arrange her furniture in a manner that appeared chic, impressive, cozy and warm, all at once.

The living room had enough space for Capri to situate her seven-piece suite in a more appealing arrangement. She had the long, gray sofa with mauve swirls placed in front of the large bay window, and she'd sat the glass coffee table in front of it. On either side of the matching armchairs in the far corner of the room, tall glass end tables had been placed. There was one bare wall where Capri decided to put the cushiony love seat. At each end of it sat tall leafy ficus plants. On the wall, above the love seat was a beautiful black-and-white painting of two lovers.

The other rooms were decorated in much the same fashion. Though Capri preferred dark colors, she still managed to give the entire house a distinctively feminine feel. Her walls were graced by her own works, though she'd saved the majority of her "racier" photographs for her bedroom.

"Capri, girl, this is so nice," Pepper said, walking down the three carpeted steps leading from the kitchen/dining room.

Capri wrapped her arms around her small frame and sighed. "I know. I'm almost speechless."

"I wouldn't mind living out here myself."

Capri's eyes widened and she took Pepper's arms. "Well, I mind, so get out."

"Oh, so that's how it is?" Pepper cried, pretending to be hurt even though she was laughing.

"You're damn straight." Capri muttered, pulling her friend along behind her. "Course you'd probably go straight next door and ask Tiberius if he wanted a roommate."

Pepper sent a devious glare in the general direction of Tiberius's house. "Now there's an idea…" she said in a frisky tone.

The two friends burst into peals of laughter and pretended to wrestle each other off the porch. A huge brick from the curving round step was loose and when Capri raced across it her foot got caught in the crack, causing her to fall.

"Cap!" Pepper yelled, kneeling beside her friend.

"What?" Capri sourly replied, easing her foot out from between the bricks.

"Damn," she hissed, frowning at the ugly scratches on her ankle.

"Girl, are you gonna be okay?"

Capri winced as she gently pulled her black cross trainer from her swelling foot. "I think so."

Pepper shook her head and helped Capri to her feet. "Let's go to the emergency room."

"Pep, I'm fine," Capri insisted, though she was barely able to stand.

"No way, something could be broken."

"I don't think so. It'll just swell up, that's all."

"I still think someone should look at it, so come on."

"Pepper—"

"No arguments. We'll take my car and I'll get you to the closest hospital."

With the excruciating pain throbbing in her foot, Capri was in no mood to argue. Putting most of her weight on Pepper, she hobbled to the car.

Chapter 5

"Mmm..." Tiberius groaned, settling his large form in one of the armchairs. He'd retreated to a deserted waiting room to take a break after leaving the delivery room. Having just helped to bring a beautiful baby girl into the world, he'd decided to take a moment to himself.

Tiberius didn't think he'd ever get used to his chosen profession. The rush he felt when he saw a new life push its way into the world—it was a sensation like no other, even though the births weren't always easy. Tonight, for instance, the baby's mother had opted for natural childbirth and her child hadn't come so smoothly. Of course, everything worked out in the end but little Charlotte Monique Fisher had succeeded in draining everyone of energy—including her doctor.

In spite of the varied and frequent joys he found in the field of obstetrics, Tiberius knew from the beginning, it had been a choice made for the sake of making a choice. Over the last twelve years, however, obstetrics had become both his purpose and his true passion. He honestly couldn't imagine himself wanting to do another thing with his professional life.

A lazy smile crossed Tiberius's mouth as he thought about his job and how much he loved it. Something phenomenal happened almost every day and he wouldn't trade it for anything. As he'd told Capri earlier, he took his work very seriously.

The satisfied grin on Tiberius's face didn't go unnoticed by Calvin Kennedy, who was passing by.

"Hey, man, what's goin' on?" Calvin asked, slapping his hand across Tiberius's shoulder.

"Nothing, just relaxing for a minute," Tiberius told his older colleague. "Just got out of the delivery room."

Calvin raised one hand and nodded. "Say no more. I assume it was a successful birth?"

"Very," Tiberius confirmed, his grin becoming wider.

"Heard you got stuck organizing Thomas's retirement festivities?"

Tiberius heard the amusement in Calvin's question. "I was honored to have been asked."

"Bull." Calvin laughed.

"No argument there," Tiberius joined in the laughter, but then shrugged. "I couldn't say no, especially when the man was so instrumental in giving a new doctor like me a shot."

"Well, you earned it, and Thomas knows talent when he sees it."

"Talent, huh?" Tiberius turned the word over in his head. "Talk to me about my talent once I've put this event together," he chuckled as Calvin slapped his shoulder.

"Well, hey, I was gonna grab a cup of coffee in the cafeteria. Care to join me?" Calvin invited.

"Ahh, what the hell," Tiberius accepted, pushing himself from his chair.

Calvin held the waiting room door open and headed for the elevators. "I just need to look in on the emergency room for a minute."

Tiberius leaned his head back against the paneled walls and pushed his hands into the deep pockets of his long white coat. "No problem."

The emergency room of Kelly Memorial was a madhouse as usual. When Pepper arrived with an injured Capri in tow, she figured it would be at least a half hour before anyone could see them.

"Can we sit down, please?" Capri whined, her pretty face darkened by a frown.

"Capri, we need to stay in line so we can get a doctor to look at your foot before it gets worse."

Capri cast a skeptical glare down at her swollen foot and sighed. "I don't think it'll get worse."

"This won't take long, man."

Tiberius smiled and waved Calvin off. "Take your time, I'll wait," he assured his friend and panned his light-brown stare around the E.R. He did a double take and frowned slightly when he saw a woman across the room who reminded him of Capri Timmons. Tiberius watched her for a second or two before he realized that it *was* Capri. When he noticed her leaning against her girlfriend Pepper, he wasted no more time heading over to her.

"Listen, I can't take this anymore. I gotta sit down," Capri cried, slapping a thick curl out of her face.

Pepper rolled her eyes and stomped her foot simultaneously. "Cap, will you—"

"What's going on? Is everything okay?"

Pepper and Capri looked up at the sound of the deep male voice bellowing overhead. "Tiberius," they said in unison.

"What are you doing here?" Tiberius asked Capri, his voice growing softer.

"She tripped and fell on a loose step," Pepper explained. "It's swelling badly and she can't even wear her shoe."

Tiberius's stare fell from Capri's face to her shoeless right foot. "Dammit," he whispered, easily lifting Capri in his arms.

"Did this happen at the house?"

"Uh…well, yes," Capri nodded, more stunned than she wanted to admit as she eased her arms around his neck.

Tiberius was able to find a couple of vacant seats in the waiting area. He sat Capri down, and knelt before her. Cupping her foot in his palms, he studied her injury.

Capri's dark eyes widened and she glanced up at Pepper. "It looks worse than it really is…jeez!" she hissed, when he pressed his thumbs against her heel.

Tiberius slid his eyes to her face and grimaced. "Does it?"

"I just needed to sit down," Capri assured him as she tried to keep from wincing at the pain.

Tiberius kept his head bowed. "You need more than that," he advised. "But I don't think it's broken."

"Tiberius, it's all right. I'm gonna be okay," Capri continued to tell him, though she found his concern quite pleasing.

"Hmm." His tone was absent and he lifted her against him once more. He managed to find a free table and left her there while he went to find someone who could help her. In minutes, an intern was seeing to her injuries.

"Well, it's swollen," the young med student, Carlos Dunston announced a while later, "but not broken. Try to keep the pressure off for a couple of days, all right?"

Capri nodded and inspected the neat wrapping job Carlos had done on her foot. "Thanks," she sighed.

Carlos nodded and spoke for a few moments with Tiberius before he left the examining space.

"I've gotta get that step fixed," Tiberius proclaimed when he returned.

"I should've been watching where I was going instead of carrying on with Pep."

"Hey!" Pepper cried.

A quick smile flashed across Tiberius's face. "Still, I've put it off way too long. I obviously can't keep ignoring it. It split shortly after the remodeling was done."

"I'm sorry," Capri said, feeling as if it was her fault.

Tiberius frowned and stepped in front of Capri. Placing his hands on either side of her on the table, he leaned in close. "I wish you'd stop blaming yourself for this. You don't need to apologize to me."

Capri was silent for a moment. Her wide eyes lowered from the intensity of his stare and she shrugged. "Thank you so much for your help."

Tiberius cupped her chin and made her look at him. "You don't need to thank me, either."

Capri's lashes almost fluttered closed and she willed herself not to swoon before him. "You won't let me apologize, you won't let me thank you. What can I do?" she asked.

"Go home and stay off that foot," Tiberius ordered, reluctantly pulling his hand away from her face. "I'll be over later to check on you."

"Oh, there's no need for you to do that," Capri argued.

"It's the least I can do," he firmly replied, ignoring her protest. "Pepper, you'll get her home?"

"Of course."

Tiberius nodded, then slid his gaze back to Capri. "I'll see you later."

Capri's dark eyes followed Tiberius as he walked away. She watched him until he was out of sight.

A small smile had brightened Pepper's face as she witnessed the interesting scene between her best friend and the handsome doctor. "Like I said, it's gonna be hard turning down a man like that for long," she whispered in Capri's ear and gave her a devilish wink.

"He saw to my foot, Pep."

"Today a foot, tomorrow…"

Capri didn't want to laugh, but there was no stopping it.

Later that evening, Capri was going over some proof sheets when her doorbell rang. Grimacing, she looked down at the oversized blue T-shirt she was wearing. The long sleeves fell well past her wrists and the hemline stopped just below the swell of her buttocks. Shrugging, she threw down the magnifying glass she carried and wobbled over to the door. Though the most painful throbbing had ceased, she still heeded the intern's warning that she keep the pressure off her leg. When she pulled the door open, Tiberius was there leaning against the doorjamb. Pressing her full lips together, Capri looked way up into the striking brown depths of his eyes.

"Look at you," Tiberius sighed, pulling her arm into a gentle hold and guiding her back to the love seat.

Capri smiled and shook her head at him. "It's a lot better than it was earlier."

Tiberius made her sit all the way back on the sofa. "I'm sure it is, but you still need to stay off of it."

"Well if I had done that, you wouldn't be in here now," she pointed out, smiling up at him.

The deep dimples at each corner of Tiberius's mouth appeared. "This is true, but at least you don't have to show me out."

Capri tossed her head back, the thick curls bouncing around her face. "You're so thoughtful."

Tiberius's deep-set eyes narrowed and he was once again struck by how lovely Capri was. Shaking his head, he pushed his hands deeply into his jeans pockets and looked around the living room. "Looks good in here. I didn't think you'd have it all together so fast."

Capri's eyes scanned the room along with his. "Well, the movers were a big help and so was Pep."

"I like it."

Capri leaned back on the sofa with her arms across her chest. "You really do? I mean, you don't think it's too dark or anything?"

Tiberius frowned a bit as he considered the question. "Uh-uh, I think it's relaxing."

"Me, too," Capri agreed, nodding.

"Especially this," Tiberius said, pointing behind Capri to the black-and-white painting of the lovers. "Did you do this?"

Capri propped her elbow on the arm of the love seat and looked up at the sensual picture. "A friend of mine painted it."

Tiberius's eyes shone with interest as he studied the piece. "Did he use live models?"

"You know, I never asked. If he did, I bet those two had a ball," Capri nodded, her dark eyes twinkling with mischief.

"Hmph, in more ways than one," Tiberius noted.

Capri burst into laughter and Tiberius joined her. Their eyes repeatedly fell to the painting and, after a while, the easy laughter died down.

Tiberius cleared his throat and took a seat on the edge of the love seat. "Let me look at this," he offered softly, lifting her foot and pulling away the fuzzy slipper she wore.

Capri pressed her shaking hands against the hem of her short T-shirt, not wanting to reveal any more than she already had. Of course, that didn't stop Tiberius's gaze from sliding over every exposed inch of her legs and thighs. His strong fingers slowly glided over the scratches on her ankle before moving on.

Capri uttered a soft gasp and Tiberius stopped the progress of his caress. Grimacing slightly, he pulled the slipper back over her foot and absently toyed with the fuzz. "Capri?"

"Mmm-hmm?"

Tiberius cut himself off when a sound resembling a deep growl reached his ears. It seemed to be coming from around the corner and it caught his otherwise undivided attention. Glancing over at Capri, he slowly nodded, "Is that *little* Lewey?"

Close to laugher, Capri nodded as well. "Yes, he probably senses someone unfamiliar in the house. Would you like to meet him?"

The look of uncertainty on Tiberius's handsome face quickly changed to one of total nervousness. "You don't have to go to any trouble," he said, his deep voice more than a little shaky.

Lewey, however, had already decided to investigate and was rounding the corner. Tiberius's narrowed gaze widened slightly when he saw the dog. Unconsciously, he inched back on the love seat.

Lewey strode into the living room like a king surveying his castle. He stopped next to the love seat and sniffed Capri's hand, before moving on to the chair's other occupant.

Man and dog studied each other intensely. Though Capri was amused by Tiberius's obvious discomfort with the monstrous-looking St. Bernard-rottweiler mix, she didn't want to prolong the agony.

"Lewey," Capri called softly, snapping her fingers, "come here, sweetie."

The large, beautiful black dog moved closer to his tiny mistress. When he was satisfied that she was safe, his attention returned to the unfamiliar visitor.

A dog lover himself, Tiberius couldn't help but study Lewey's shiny black coat and huge features. Turning his head slowly so he wouldn't excite Lewey, Tiberius glanced at Capri. "I can't get over how gorgeous he is. Or how big."

"Thanks, his mother was a rottweiler and his father was a St. Bernard," Capri explained.

"No wonder," Tiberius whispered. "You think he'll mind if I pet him?"

"No, if he hasn't bitten your arm off by now, he won't."

An uncertain grin crossed Tiberius's mouth. "That makes me feel so much better."

Lewey obviously understood or felt that Tiberius had complimented him, for he allowed the man to pet him. He licked Tiberius's hand, showing his approval of the big man seated next to his owner.

Tiberius's rich laughter filled the room in response to Lewey appreciating his hand. "He's friendly."

"Hmph, for a change. He must like you."

"Well I like him…and his owner."

For the next several seconds Tiberius and Capri held each other's gazes. Each wanted to say something, but neither made the first move. Luckily, the heavy mood was interrupted by the sound of the doorbell.

Tiberius pulled his eyes away and shook his head as if to clear it. "I'll get it."

Kiva was on the other side of the door. When she saw Tiberius, her large brown eyes widened. "Well, hello stranger!"

"What the hell are you doin' here?" Tiberius exclaimed, pulling Kiva close for a tight hug. "I didn't know you were friends with Capri."

"Mmm-hmm," Kiva replied, smoothing her hands across Tiberius's wide back, "she and Rod have been friends forever so of course we are, too."

A smirk added a devilish element to Tiberius's handsome face. "Yeah, just like him not to introduce me before now."

Kiva laughed, but didn't respond. Instead, she walked on into the house. Spotting Capri on the sofa with her foot bandaged, she frowned. "What in the world happened to you?"

"I tripped on a step," Capri explained. "I was showing Pepper out of the house and we were laughing and…"

"You were the one who was trippin'?" Kiva noted, causing Tiberius and Capri to laugh. Kiva knelt to pet Lewey then looked around the living room. "Capri, this is so nice. I love what you've done so far."

"Thanks, I was able to do so much more with it since there's so much more room here than I had at the condo."

"Well, I think it's fabulous."

"So do I. I plan on being here for a while," Capri admitted, feeling very comfortable in her new surroundings.

Kiva smiled and glanced at Tiberius, whose unwavering gaze

had never left Capri's face. "I guess you're glad to hear that, huh, Tibe?"

"Hmm?… What?" he muttered, looking over at Kiva after a moment.

"Sounds like you'll have a permanent resident," Kiva clarified, amused by how absorbed the man seemed by Capri.

"Oh…yeah," Tiberius finally came to his senses.

"Steady cash flow," Kiva teased, rubbing her hands together in a sneaky manner.

"You're crazy," Capri accused through laughter.

Suddenly, Tiberius cleared his throat and ran both hands through his thick, curly crop of hair.

"Um, I better get goin', ladies," he announced, his eyes settling back on Capri's face. "I'll see you tomorrow," he promised, before smirking at Kiva. "All right, girl, holler at Rod for me."

"Will do!" Kiva shouted, never missing the intense look on Tiberius's handsome face when he looked at Capri.

"So what do you think of your new landlord?" she asked when she was sure he had gone.

"He's very nice."

"Yeah?"

Capri groaned and rolled her dark eyes toward the ceiling. "All right, he's gorgeous and sexy as hell, but I got a feeling he's something of a…playboy, for lack of a better word."

Kiva stood from the armchair and dusted both hands across her long, form-fitting denim dress. "Honey, *playboy* is the perfect word for Tiberius Evans. He can be hard to resist though, and I got the girlfriends that'll testify to that."

"I seriously doubt that I'm his type, Kiva."

"Why not? You're a woman, aren't you?"

Capri clicked her teeth. "You know what I mean. There are obvious reasons why it couldn't work between us."

Kiva appeared clueless. "Such as?"

Sitting up a bit on the sofa, Capri let her shock show. "For starters, I'm supposed to be *saving myself,* remember?" She twisted her lips as the fact rattled something inside her. "Anyway, I've got the feeling our gorgeous doctor hates the idea of commitment."

"True," Kiva eased a hand into the pocket of her dress and paced the living room. "But have you told him that he's living next door to a virgin?"

"No! Hell no!"

Kiva raised her hands. "Well then, honey, to our gorgeous doctor you're just like any other woman. His for the taking."

Capri shook her head. "He's not really that bad. Is he?"

"Tibe's a sweetie," Kiva conceded, coming to join Capri on the sofa, "but he's a man who thrives on a challenge, and damn if you wouldn't be the perfect one."

"Oh, I don't doubt that for a minute," Capri quickly responded and her lashes briefly fluttered as she remembered the feel of his fingers along her skin. Shaking her head, she tried to clear her mind of the sensual thoughts. "Anyway, I've got a feeling that this challenge wouldn't exactly be Dr. Evans' cup of tea."

Chapter 6

Late the next morning, Capri awoke to strange sounds outside. Unmindful of the revealing cotton-gauze chemise she wore, she headed right downstairs. The closer she got to the front door, the louder the sounds of chainsaws and hammers became. Not about to open the door, Capri pulled back the long mauve drapes covering the bay window and peeked out. It appeared that someone had hired a construction crew and not informed her. There were at least eight men out front and it seemed they were relaying the entire porch.

Tiberius's promise to fix the broken step immediately came to mind. Capri was sure a mistake was being made and was about to head next door. She detoured up the small stairway and went to the dining room. Opening the long blinds over the French doors there, she looked to see if Tiberius had already left for the day.

"Tiberius!" she called, spotting him about to settle into his truck.

He had just thrown his briefcase into the truck when he heard his name. Smoothing his hand across the tan suede vest he'd put on over a long-sleeve cream shirt, he frowned and walked closer to the gate.

"Tibe!" Capri shouted again, when she saw him right next to the gate. When he looked over at her house, she waved him over.

He wasted no time getting across the yard. A look of concern darkened his handsome face when he stepped through the French doors Capri held open. His fierce expression changed to one of sensual shock when he saw what she was wearing.

"What's wrong?" he whispered, his light eyes trailing across her caramel skin seductively revealed by the skimpy attire.

Capri pointed behind her. "All those men on my porch…"

Tiberius sent a blank stare her way, before he threw his head back. "Oh…well I promised you I'd get that step fixed."

"But they're redoing the entire porch," Capri pointed out.

Tiberius was barely paying attention to the conversation because he was so entranced by Capri's dark hair. He wondered if it was as soft as it looked. Suddenly grimacing, Tiberius pushed his hands into the deep pockets of his cream trousers and glared at her. "Listen, Capri, I can't take a chance on anything else happening because of repairs that need to be made, all right?"

Capri absently toyed with the low ruffled neckline of her gown and shook her head. "Do you go to such lengths for all your tenants?"

Tiberius's strong fingers brushed against the satiny skin above the gown's neckline. Then, he took her hand in his. "No, not all. Just for the very lovely, tiny ones."

Capri's enchanting gaze widened slightly at his smooth compliment. Before she could respond though, Tiberius was gone.

"Hey, Charlie? Could you get Max to check the lighting in that corner? I think it's a little too dark."

"Sure thing, Cap."

Capri had felt up to going back to work after only one day of rest. The deadline for the cologne ad would be upon her soon enough and she didn't want to waste any more time. While she took care of last-minute details in the studio, however, her thoughts unwillingly drifted to Tiberius.

She had tried to pretend since they met that she felt nothing for him. Only to herself could she begin to admit her intense attraction to the man. Her body reacted whenever he was around.

She began to tap her magnifying glass to the easel as Tiberius completely took over her thoughts. She couldn't help but think about what she'd confessed to Pepper that day over lunch. It was the first time she'd ever admitted having reservations about her decisions to abstain. The words she spoke to Pepper had sounded almost foreign to her ears.

It went without saying that these *reservations* would have to be dealt with. If, in fact, her vow to remain a virgin had less to do with celibacy and saving herself for marriage and more to do with some expectation of herself to be more like her sisters, then she had some serious soul-searching to do.

Her attraction to Tiberius Evans was dangerous, for she could very easily give in to the increasing demands her body was insisting she satisfy. Caught in the midst of such temptation while trying to come to grips with what she really wanted could have her throwing caution, and other things, to the wind.

Capri was so absorbed in her thoughts of the handsome physician that she didn't notice Avery Erickson come into the studio.

"Earth to Capri," Avery sang, grinning when her lovely dark eyes snapped up to his face.

"I'm so sorry. I didn't even hear you come in." Capri hoped she didn't look as flustered as she felt.

Avery waved his hand. "No problem, but you look like there's somethin' heavy on your mind," he detected, gazing appreciatively at her small form encased in a denim jean jumper.

Capri was oblivious to his stare. "Well, work always keeps me in an uproar," she sighed.

"Is it the ad?"

"The deadline will be here before we know it."

"You know what you need?" Avery said, pulling the camera Capri was holding out of her hands and turning her to face him. "You need to get out."

"You think so?" Capri asked, her full lips twitching slightly.

"I do."

Capri walked away from Avery. She gave him a mischievous look over her shoulder. "And I suppose you're offering?"

Avery spread his arms wide. "If you insist."

"Well, I don't," Capri declined gaily and with her brightest smile in place. "Look, Avery, maybe I didn't make this clear before but I try very hard not to get involved with the people I work with. Especially the models. No offense."

The confident gleam in Avery's dark eyes dimmed. "Well what's wrong with models?"

"Avery, I just don't mix work and play, all right?"

Tapping his fingers against his square jaw, Avery took a moment to think. "Okay then, we'll just have to wait until after our work is done to play."

Capri tossed a thick curl out of her eye and tilted her head back to look directly at the tall, attractive man across from her. "Forget it Avery," she said politely but firmly, although she didn't think it would be the end of his pursuit.

Aside from Avery being late, the first shoot went off without any serious problems. Capri couldn't believe that she hadn't used half the time she'd anticipated for the shoot. She'd sent one of her assistants off to prepare her darkroom, so she could get started right away on the prints.

"All right everybody, that was a good one! We'll meet on the beach at 6:00 a.m. sharp! You guys know where."

Everyone groaned at the early hour, but they were glad to have the rest of the day off. Avery decided to make one last attempt with Capri and walked up behind her. He pulled out one of his cards and held it in front of her face.

"What's this?" Capri asked, frowning slightly at the gray card with raised black letters.

Avery waited until Capri turned to face him to continue. "Call me when you think you can relax your rules."

Capri glanced at the card and then watched Avery saunter away.

Shaking her head at his determination, she slid his card into her bag.

Deciding not to waste any time, Capri went right to work developing the prints from the day's shoot. She was very pleased with her work, as well as with the group she was working with.

"Now all I need to do is decide which prints to include in the portfolio," she whispered to herself pushing her hands into the back pockets of her jumper.

"Can you hold off on that a little while?"

Capri dropped the prints on the table and turned around. "Hey, what are you doing here?"

Rod stepped from the shadows of the doorway. "I need your help."

"For what?"

"I need to go shopping."

"Shopping?"

"Shopping."

Totally confused, Capri leaned back against the table. "Am I missing something?"

Rod came close to Capri and held her upper arms in a light hold. "You gotta keep quiet about this, all right?"

"Uh-huh. What is it?"

"I'm gonna propose to Kiva, but I need an engagement ring and—"

Capri's screaming interrupted.

"Will you hush?" Rod ordered, clamping his hand across Capri's mouth.

Capri nodded but her dark eyes were impossibly wide with excitement.

"I need some help picking the thing out. You think you can help without tellin' the whole building?"

Capri pulled Rod's hand away and gave him a dazzling smile. "You can count on me."

She threw her arms about his neck and hugged him tight.

Chapter 7

Capri stood in her yard with a puzzled look on her face. For the third time since she pulled into her driveway, she'd glanced next door at Tiberius's house. She'd been standing at the passenger side of her truck gathering portfolios when she'd heard the angry voices.

Capri tried to ignore the heated argument next door, but it was no use. She could tell that Tiberius was obviously into it with a very unhappy woman. Her voice was high-pitched and she was practically screaming.

Of course, nosiness finally won out. Capri grabbed the rest of her portfolios and padded across the yard. She stood next to the high wooden fence surrounding the back of Tiberius's house and listened.

"You are such a bastard, Tiberius."

"You knew that before we slept together."

"I can't believe I was so stupid. Sleeping with a man just because he looks good? I must be crazy."

"Well, that's exactly why I slept with you and I don't feel crazy," Tiberius threw back.

"Why am I not surprised?"

Tiberius paused. "Clarissa, did you think that just because we had sex it meant we were in a relationship?"

"Tibe, I—"

"Yes or no?" Tiberius softly coaxed.

"I thought we'd build on something. I'd be lying if I said otherwise."

A short laugh came from Tiberius. "You thought a heavy

relationship would come from a one-night stand? You knew that's what it'd be when you came home with me."

Through her sobbing, Clarissa tried to answer. "We had sex *more* than once...but you're making it sound like something so much cheaper. Yes, I figured something steady could come from it—there was a connection. I guess I took it more seriously than you."

"Then I'm sorry, that's where you made your mistake. And for you still to harp on this...it's been over a year."

"Right! And there were plenty of women afterward to blur your memory of me, I'm sure! To you I was nothing more than a tenant for your grandma's cottage. A tenant with benefits."

Suddenly, the gate wrenched open and Clarissa ran right into Capri, scattering portfolios everywhere.

"I'm so sorry," Clarissa whispered, kneeling to help Capri gather her books.

"Are you going to be all right?" Capri asked, taking in the woman's red eyes and tear-stained cheeks.

Clarissa wiped the tears from her eyes and shoved the portfolios at Capri. "Tiberius is a cold son of a bitch," she grumbled.

Capri gave Clarissa a small smile. "That's hard to believe."

Clarissa focused her hard glare on Capri. "Watch out for that guy in there, girl. If ever there was a man who only wanted a woman for sex, it's Doctor Tiberius Evans."

Capri watched Clarissa stand and head down the driveway to her car. Looking at the gate, Capri debated for a moment whether to go inside to see Tiberius. Finally, she decided against it.

Tiberius didn't want to acknowledge the sinking feeling in the pit of his stomach when he saw Capri leaving the elevator with Jaye Horace. The new doctor looked just a bit too cozy with Capri for his liking.

"Jaye, callin' it quits for the day?"

Capri blinked at the sound of Tiberius's voice and looked up as the beginnings of a smile began across her mouth.

"Actually, I just removed the last of Ms. Timmons's bandages and everything's looking just fine." Jaye's dark face shone with pride and something a bit more animal.

Tiberius rolled his eyes and didn't bother to point out that Jaye was looking nowhere in the vicinity of Capri's foot.

"So, are you done here?" Tiberius was taking Capri's elbow even as he spoke.

Jaye laid a hand across Tiberius's shirt sleeve. "I was just about to see Ms. Timmons to her car."

"Don't bother. I'm guessing there're a lot of other patients you need to see to," Tiberius said as he sent a sly wink in his colleague's direction and pulled Capri away with him.

She waited until they'd located her car in the mammoth parking deck before speaking, "If you don't like Jaye you really should be a little more obvious about it. He might get the wrong idea."

Tiberius picked up on her dig and didn't bother to deny it. "Only idea he had was to get you into bed."

"Yeah, I caught that." Capri set her things onto the backseat of her Pathfinder. She saw the surprise in his eyes when she looked at him. "What? I guess it's not about that for you, huh?"

"In most cases," Tiberius folded his arms across his chest and leaned against the hood of the SUV. "At least I'm up front about it."

"Ah…and it's best to be up front rather than waste time trying to woo the woman?" Capri asked, though she couldn't resist admiring the breadth of his muscular arms bared by the short-sleeved shirt he wore.

Grimacing, Tiberius scanned the sun-drenched parking deck and shrugged. "Wooing just leads to misunderstandings."

"And are you speaking from experience?"

"More than I wish I had."

Capri pushed up and down on her toes once. "Maybe it's time for you to change your techniques. Maybe be a little less obvious?" She suggested playfully.

"You'd want a guy like that?" Tiberius was serious, suddenly fixing her with a probing look. "Honestly? You'd want someone who beat around the bush and acted like he didn't want you when wanting you was all he could think of?"

"Well…" Capri followed Tiberius's lead and leaned against her vehicle. "Seeing as how that's the only type of man I've been attracting lately, I'd be willing to set my sights on a different type of guy."

Tiberius burst into laughter that had him doubling over. Capri could practically read his thoughts when he looked up at her.

"Go on and say it," she permitted.

"All right…*women*."

His laughter returned and she was struck by the appeal of his expression. "So would you be kind enough to give me more detail on that, Doctor?" She worked to take her mind off the crazy somersaults being performed in her stomach.

"Okay," Tiberius stroked his jaw as though concentrating on how best to state his argument. "Women claim to want a man who'll wine, dine and romance them, and then they realize it was all about sex for the guy. Then they feel betrayed. If the poor bastard would've just been up front about what he wanted in the first place everyone would be a lot happier."

"Everyone except the poor bastard," Capri noted, grateful when the sun dipped behind a heavy cloud and provided shade. "But I don't know if I'd agree with your reasoning. I can't buy that many women would accept an offer just for sex—even if it would be more honest just to be up front about wanting it."

"Hmm," Tiberius massaged his neck and considered her point of view. "There're a lot of women in the world, *Ms.* Timmons. Anyway, I'd rather be up front and *not* get what I want than hide it and suffer consequences later." He massaged a sudden pain that streaked through his forehead. "Hell, even when you *are* up front, the chances of suffering consequences are still pretty high."

Now Capri was frowning, too. "Sounds like most of your experiences have been bad."

"Not all, but enough to jade me, I guess." Tiberius remembered his conversation with his older colleague, Oscar Addison, then.

Silence settled between them and Tiberius realized he'd lost track of the time talking to Capri. The sun began to beam down again and he pushed off the truck to open the driver's-side door.

"Sorry for holding your ears hostage." He helped settle her behind the wheel. "I know your work is very active but you should rest that foot as much as possible anyway."

"All right." Capri allowed herself just a few more moments to gawk at him.

"I'll be over later to check on you."

"Oh, Tibe, you don't have to—"

"I'll be over later."

Without arguing the point, Capri started the ignition and left the parking lot. Tiberius watched her leave and told himself to forget about it. He'd go check on her as any concerned doctor would, and that would be that. He'd had enough of mixing neighbors with pleasure.

"So does anyone know what Avery's excuse was for being late to the shoot this time?"

Everyone laughed over Capri's question. She'd offered to treat her crew that afternoon and they were enjoying a working lunch at a small, unassuming restaurant not far from her new neighborhood.

"Got a sick aunt who lives out in Kendall," Barry Coines spoke between bites of his broiled scallops. "Said he had to go see her and got tied up with things. He's her closest relative."

"And how many of us believe that?" Capri took a poll of the group after silence surrounded the table for the better part of fifteen seconds.

"That's cold, Capri."

She flashed a wink at her assistant. "I didn't say he was lying."

"But you don't buy it?"

Capri popped another popcorn shrimp into her mouth. "I'd probably buy it a lot faster if he'd said there was a sick ex-girlfriend who needed him to make her chicken soup and he was her closest lover."

The group roared with laughter drawing interested glances from Tiberius and his friends, who were also dining at the restaurant. The newly formed retirement committee had decided to meet for a weekend lunch at the same seafood bar.

Losing whatever interest he had in the staid conversation at his own table, Tiberius focused in on Capri. He had to smile at himself for likening her to some sugary treat atop a cake. But, God, she was lovely with her curls pinned haphazardly upon her head and the candy-pink tennis dress that molded to her lush curves while leaving her toned arms and legs enticingly bare. The dainty amethyst anklet she wore simply beckoned an onlooker to her tiny feet encased in white slide-in sneakers.

He was more pleased than he realized to see her there. The SeaBar was in the shopping outlet exclusive to their development and frequented by most everyone who lived there. He'd told her how good the food was and hoped she'd give it a try. Judging from the amount of laughter roaring from her table, he figured they were enjoying the food. Of course, he also wondered when any of them might have had the chance to take a bite.

She was a mystery, he thought, with the face and body of a goddess. She didn't seem to flaunt them though. Tugging on the hem of his gray polo shirt, he shifted in his seat and observed her lunch partners. Probably coworkers, he thought. He hoped.

Anyway, she didn't seem the type who would flaunt her lovers either. There was something almost, innocent, about her. He kept coming back to that word and shook off the assumption yet again. Still, it niggled at him and he didn't know why. Besides…neighbors and pleasure didn't mix and he'd be just fine with never knowing why.

He'd have to be.

"Tibe, is this gonna work for you? Tibe?"

Tiberius's resulting stare clearly prompted further explanation. Monroe Wilkins grinned and tapped a finger to the diagram on the paper. "We figure delegating tasks to everyone will make the meetings more productive and push this thing further along."

Smiling at the eager anesthesiologist, Tiberius made an effort to browse the detailed drawing. Then, closing his eyes, he massaged the bridge of his nose. "Something's just not clicking for me about this, guys. The thing seems…dry, stale." He pushed the page across the table. "The man's retiring. He should be thinking about everything he's accomplished and what's still in store for him instead of it seeming like the end of the road. These *tasks* have 'end of the road' written all over them."

"So give us some specifics here. What's the best way to handle this?"

Tiberius met Sara Kramer's inquiry with a slow shrug. "I haven't got a clue."

The pediatrician laughed, and soon everyone else at the table joined in.

"You know, I think we've beat this horse long enough. Anyone object to adjourning here?"

Tiberius's suggestion was met with a round of agreement. The group cleared out without a moment of hesitation. Capri was finishing up her lunch appointment and noticed Tiberius motioning for the check.

"Could I interest you in walking back with me?" she asked, smiling when he looked up at her.

"Hey," his baritone voice was soft as he stood. "Yeah, yeah, that'd be good." He winced a little then and glanced down at her sneakers. "Actually I drove my gas guzzler. You sure you're up for walking on that foot?"

Capri knew then that had her injury been truly serious the man would've probably forbidden her ever to walk again. "I think I'll be all right, Doctor. Shall we?"

"So how'd you like the SeaBar?" Tiberius asked once they'd set out for the short walk back to their respective homes.

"It was great. I actually may never eat at another seafood place." In the short time she'd lived at Seaside Trace, Capri had come to realize that the area wasn't as stark and intimidating as she'd once believed. The residents were friendly, open, and seemed to treasure the fact that theirs was a walking community. The day, of course, was sunny and warm, but it was the cyclists, skaters and walkers that truly added to the brightness of the neighborhood. Capri gave herself a mental pat on the back. Her decision to move had been a fine one indeed.

"Stop."

"I'm serious."

"You and your friends didn't appear to be eating much." Tiberius hid his hands in his pockets and hoped she didn't catch on to how curious he was.

"I promise you we all enjoyed it and there's *always* loads of rowdiness when I go out with my crew."

"Your crew?"

"My photography crew." Capri switched her camera bag to her other shoulder. "We were discussing one of our models."

Tiberius wouldn't let himself dwell on the fact that her clarification made him feel much better. "So what's your job like?"

"Ha! Full of prima donnas. Mostly male ones."

Tiberius laughed. "So, do you ever regret being behind the camera instead of in front of it?"

"No." Capri took a deep breath and enjoyed the shadows cast by the tall palms lining the sea. "Photography fascinates me. I truly believe in the phrase 'the camera doesn't lie.' In the perfect shot there's a raw beauty that...I don't know...it captivates me."

"So are you captivated by *all* your subjects?" Again, Tiberius hoped she couldn't tell what he really wanted to know.

"Captivated? By *my* subjects? No, lately no," she quickly stated and joined him in laughter. "The joy for me is working until I come across the few who *do* captivate me." She slanted Tiberius a glance. "I wouldn't mind shooting you sometime."

"Forget it." He waved a hand about his head. "I could never compete with those guys who pose for you."

In truth, Capri thought, those guys could never compete with him. She took a moment to observe him again and the rest of the walk passed in sweet silence.

Capri's voice echoed loudly in the air when her musical accompaniment was shut down in mid chorus. She whipped her head around to find Tiberius standing near the MP3 player she'd carried out to the patio.

"What are you doing?" His expression was curious and awed as he watched her.

Capri waved a hand toward her soapy Pathfinder. "Isn't it obvious?"

"What about that foot?"

"Do you recall how long ago that was?"

"And here you are doing something else dangerous."

"It was only a few scratches and, as you said yourself, it was long past time you had that step repaired." She slapped the sponge to the roof of the truck.

Tiberius had already zoned out of her explanation as her attire struck him speechless. The cutoffs and bikini top held him entranced. He didn't even realize he'd been gawking until he tuned into her calling his name.

"I don't feel right about you on that foot, a few scratches or not."

Capri judged her position atop the SUV. "Technically I'm not *on* it, you know?"

"Right," he watched as she continued the scrubbing chore. "You should let me do that," he said when she caught him staring again.

"Tibe...for the last time, I'm fine."

"I believe you but you're only spreading around the dirt the way you're doing it."

"I've done this before."

"Then don't you think it's time you learned how to do it right?" he smirked.

"All right." She threw the sponge at his chest and smiled when he fielded it easily before it hit his T-shirt. "So what do you suggest, Doc?"

"First..." Surprising, exasperating and amusing her, he effortlessly plucked her from the roof of the car and sat her to her feet.

There was no arguing that his elbow grease was far more powerful than hers. But rather than stroke his ego further, she kept all compliments to herself.

"So should I be a good little girl and go get refreshments?" she asked instead.

Tiberius overlooked her sarcasm on purpose. "Now you're learning."

Capri waited until he'd turned back to scrubbing and then doused his back with the bucket of soapy water.

Tiberius took his revenge swiftly and in moments he had her on her back and begging for mercy as he tickled her.

Capri pretended to lose her breath as she pleaded. The second he eased off, she grabbed the hose and sprayed him square in the face.

Tiberius relieved her of the hose easily and repaid the favor tenfold. Soon Capri's hair was a mass of limp coils and everything was wet. It was all in fun, but amidst the play and laughter, their bodies betrayed them.

With Tiberius sprawled between her thighs, she could feel every bit of his chiseled length. There was no mistaking his arousal, hard and heavy against the middle of her cutoffs. His chest was a granite slab presently outlined beneath his soaked white T-shirt. Capri couldn't resist the temptation to knead his flexing pecs and arched into the rigid abs sealed against her stomach.

The moment was just as arousing for Tiberius who relished the feel of her ample breasts rising against him almost as much as the sight of her nipples deliciously rigid beneath her soaked bikini top. The front ties of the racy garment had come loose during their play and the material barely covered the part of her he was almost desperate to see.

Bowing his head, he uttered a brief prayer to request more willpower and then he pushed off her.

"You should, um…you should go change out of those…those clothes…" He cleared his throat. "Before you catch a cold to go along with that bruised foot."

Capri nodded and let him help her to her feet. "Well, thanks… for the help."

"Any time." He pushed a hand through his dark hair while continually raking his light eyes across her. She could barely keep the ties closed over her full chest. When she mercifully left him alone, he reached for the hose and gave himself a quick cold shower.

"Looking good," Pepper remarked as she strolled into Capri's kitchen a few days later.

Capri only sipped from her coffee mug and waited for Pepper to continue, knowing remarks on the loveliness of the home weren't the only thing she was bursting to comment on.

"Had dinner with the good doctor lately?"

"No, I haven't seen him in a few days actually."

Now it was Pepper's turn to wait for further comment.

"Not since he came over to wash my car."

Folding her arms over her black halter, Pepper nodded in satisfaction. "Now this is conversation worth driving all the way out here for. Dish."

"Nothing happened...well, nothing much."

"How much?"

"Pepper..."

"You like him. What's wrong with that?" Pepper took her place at the table and fixed Capri with confused eyes.

"You know why, you've seen him. You've met him."

"Right, not only is he gorgeous, but he's intelligent and he's decent."

Capri topped off her coffee and came to join Pepper at the table. "The only problem is he still strikes me as a playboy."

Pepper laughed. "Newsflash, hon, but there's no way a man can look that way and not fall victim to playing that role at least once in his lifetime."

"Which makes him dangerous."

"Why? Because he's got you questioning certain decisions you've made about your body and who you've decided to give it to?"

"You pretty much hit that one on the head."

"I'm not a bartender for nothing."

Capri held her head in her hands. "I'm doing more than questioning, Pep. I'm imagining, daydreaming about..." She winced as a few of those images popped into her mind.

Pepper only leaned across the table to pat the top of her best friend's head.

* * *

Capri had always enjoyed taking time out to plant. She'd often indulged in the activity and her former condo, had resembled a veritable greenhouse before she moved. The pots of gaily colored flowers decorating her condo, however, couldn't compare to the feel of toiling away in her very own garden. Capri finally managed time to plant some bulbs around her house. She was having a marvelous Saturday morning working in the rich soil, but welcomed the company from Lewey and the friend he brought along.

"Does your dad know you're over here, miss?" Capri asked Droopey and laughed when the lovely collie bounded over to cover her arm in licks.

"All right, all right I'll keep quiet!" Capri giggled.

The dogs must have believed her for they left Capri to her gardening and went about their frolicking a short distance away.

"Droop?"

Capri smiled but continued her work when she heard his voice.

"Droopey? Where are you?"

"Looks like the jig's up, girl," Capri warned.

"Droop?"

"She's okay." Capri waited for Tiberius to emerge around her side of the house.

"She bothering you?" Tiberius asked as he noticed her gardening.

Capri hesitated, taking stock of her work. "Sorry about this, I um…didn't bother to ask before I started to plant these things."

Tiberius grinned. "You never had to ask me that anyway."

"So it's all right?"

"Very all right. This is your home and you can do whatever you like to put your own mark on it. Well, anything except drawing a big red *C* on the roof, that is."

Capri snapped her fingers. "Guess I'll need to cancel the painting crew that was heading over this afternoon." Her laughter softened.

"Thanks, Tibe." She watched him shrug and then she took another look at her work. "I hope it'll be a good mark. I'm really only experimenting here."

"I think you'll have positive results." Tiberius eased a hand into a side pocket of his walnut-brown trousers.

"I'm still a novice at this so I'm afraid my gardening skills are nowhere near as primed as whoever you paid to do *your* yard."

"Now I'm really offended." Tiberius pressed a hand to the front of his crisp mocha shirt and fixed her with a pained look. "Are you saying I couldn't do that myself?"

"Well I didn't mean to—" Capri stopped herself when she looked up and noticed him smirking. She slapped his leg in response to his teasing.

"So, what are these?" Tiberius knelt to expect more closely.

"Bulbs. They come in their own special packet. You only need to plant it as is and water it. Then move them out here once the roots grow."

"Lemme see one of those."

Capri moved to grab the last packet which was snatched up by Lewey just as her fingers grazed it. "Sorry," she gasped amidst the laughter that fluttered in response to the dog's play.

Tiberius couldn't have cared less. He was far too taken by Capri in that moment. Without a care for his clothes or the meeting he was already late for, he tugged upon the hem of her T-shirt and gently settled her into the grass. A deep kiss followed.

Capri's response was eager as she met the deep lunges of his tongue with a force of her own. Wantonly, she arched into a soft bow when his fingers plied her firming nipples with merciless manipulation.

"Tibe…" Her voice quivered when he ground his powerful frame against her.

He broke the kiss then, and his mouth journeyed along the satin line of her cheek, jaw, neck…and farther still across the rise of her breasts and beneath the snug fabric covering her chest. She thrust her hips hard, shamelessly erotic beneath him when he rooted his lips against her top and suckled her nipples.

Tiberius's hands skirted over and under her clothes. They moved to curve about her bottom where he caressed the lush curve visible thanks to the hem of her black shorts. Capri felt him groan into her mouth and knew he'd discovered she wore nothing beneath. She tugged at his bottom lip, relishing the pleasure of his fingers on her bare skin. She whimpered his name when they brushed the petals of her sex.

The sound of her voice brought Tiberius to his senses. He uttered a sharp curse and thought about where they were, sprawled out in her yard where anyone could happen upon them. She deserved better than that. She deserved better than him.

Capri pushed herself up and watched as he called for his dog and left without another word.

Capri stopped second-guessing herself and rang the bell. It had been a few days since she'd seen Tiberius and she admitted to herself that she had missed him.

The bell went unanswered, but the Navigator was parked at its familiar angle in the driveway, so chances were good that he was still here. Setting her head at a determined angle she decided to bite the bullet and push onward.

Success. She found Tiberius on a lounge on his patio. He appeared to be frowning over a folder he held and Capri felt what little courage she'd mustered seep away then. He looked too busy to be bothered, she told herself, and was in the midst of backing away when Droopey caught sight of her and barked happily.

"I didn't want to disturb you," she explained with a painful wince when he looked up.

"No, no, you didn't." He was already setting aside the folder.

Capri was struck. She could only think of how adorable he was in the gold-rimmed glasses he was wearing.

"Come on over." Tiberius was more grateful for the interruption than he realized.

Capri raised the basket she carried. "Cookies. I bake a lot for my crew, but this is a new recipe." She pulled the paisley-print cloth from the basket. "I was hoping you'd tell me what you think before I give any to them."

"Using me for a guinea pig, eh?"

"Well, a landlord's gotta be good for something." She laughed.

"Stay," Tiberius ordered Droopey, who had already sniffed the incredible aroma of the baked treats. Droopey obeyed, though her eyes were fixed on the braided white basket and her tail thumped the ground in protest.

Tiberius helped himself to one of the warm cookies. Flavors of oatmeal, cinnamon, chocolate and a hint of something he couldn't identify, all burst to life and then melted on his tongue.

"Unbelievable. You actually made these?"

Capri was beaming. "I did."

"From scratch?"

"In that very kitchen." She hooked a thumb across her shoulder in the direction of her home.

Tiberius finished the cookie in record time and reached for another. *Washes her own car, gardens, bakes from scratch...what more could you want?*

"Thanks, Capri," he said while silently ordering the voice in his head to stow it. "I'm sure your crew deserves those, but I'll pay any price to keep the rest."

"Don't trouble yourself. They're yours." She lifted the basket. "That's why I came over." Setting the treats on the glass table near his lounge, she was about to move away when his hand circled her wrist.

"I'm sorry…for the other day. I guess I wasn't acting much different than those guys you've been trying to get away from."

Capri didn't bother to tell him that she hadn't been trying to get away from him. "It's all right." She slapped a hand to the side of her denim overalls. "We shouldn't have tension between us. Not being neighbors and all."

"I appreciate you saying that." He blinked then, as if realizing he still wore the glasses. Clearing his throat, he removed them quickly and bowed his head. "Are neighbors, um…allowed to offer invites to retirement parties?"

"Hmm…" Capri folded her arms over her chest. "Yours?"

He chuckled and leaned back on the lounge. "If you've discovered a way to retire at thirty-three please let me know."

"No such luck," she said once they'd laughed for a solid forty-five seconds.

"It's for the chief doctor at my hospital. We're gonna have another event for him at a later time, but this is a shindig that his wife's putting together at their estate."

"An estate…does that mean I can dress up outrageously?"

Tiberius stroked his jaw and pretended to consider it. "It's an elaborate estate on Key Biscayne, so I'd say dressing up outrageously is essential."

Capri clapped her hands. "In that case, I accept."

The neighbors spent the rest of the afternoon pigging out on the delicious cookies. Tiberius provided the milk.

Chapter 8

Alan Thomas was a beloved father, husband, friend, doctor and colleague mostly because of his easily approachable and down-to-earth manner. Still, the house he owned in Key Biscayne said anything but "down-to-earth."

The jaw-dropping estate gave the word *palatial* a whole new meaning. It was complete with a set of elaborate fountains in both the front and back yards. The stables boasted two Derby winners and there were separate yet equally elaborate quarters for the house staff of twenty-two. It was well known that the Thomases threw a soiree like no other. Since the event that afternoon was in honor of the king of the castle, nothing was spared.

It took Tiberius and Capri at least twenty minutes to cross into the foyer once they'd arrived. Though still early in his career, Tiberius knew and seemed comfortable around a great many of the doctors in attendance. Capri asked him about that.

"My grandmother gave money to almost every hospital in this portion of the state. I've known most of these people since long before I ever thought about becoming a doctor."

"Your grandmother sounds like she was quite a lady," Capri noted as they followed the slow-moving line through the massive marble-floored foyer.

Tiberius's handsome features softened with the memory. "She was incredible. My grandfather's construction business put in him league with most of the big wigs down here." He checked the inside pocket of his three-quarter-length, mushroom-colored suit coat and withdrew their invitation. "She refused to be a piece of arm jewelry and got busy making a name for herself as well. An invitation to a party by Tiberius and Janice Evans was as coveted as one to Alan and Felicity Thomas."

Capri was riveted as she listened to the story. Clearly, the man loved and missed his grandparents. "You were very close to them, huh?"

"They were like my parents." Tiberius pressed a hand to the small of Capri's back, left bare by the cut of her dress. The floor-length frock was stunning, to say the very least. The oval keyhole cut in the bodice offered fleeting yet tantalizing glimpses of the curve of her full breasts. Tiberius blinked away and focused on the conversation at hand. "My *actual* parents were usually off somewhere traveling for business. It wasn't until I got older that I realized all those business trips were just excuses to stay away from each other."

Capri didn't expect to hear the dark edge suddenly coloring his voice, and was thankful that they were approaching their hosts.

Whether or not Tiberius had grown up around most of the big shots in attendance, she had to admit there was a natural ease in the way he handled them. He was a man confident in his abilities and the accomplishments made in his still-budding career.

Capri would've been more surprised to discover that she added a great deal of oomph to Tiberius's popularity that day. Of course he was well-known and well-liked. Most everyone had taken him under their wing at one time or another. But Tiberius knew from the interest in his male colleagues' gazes that they had ulterior motives for calling him over to chat. And how could he blame them for wanting to speak to the beauty on his arm? It was a wonder he'd even made it out the front door with her when he picked her up.

The chic designer dress she wore clung to her petite curvaceous form like a second skin. The coral material held a shimmer that accentuated the healthy gleam of her honey-colored skin. The bodice kept his stare from straying and kept him praying for just a glimpse of the full, perfectly rounded breasts beneath.

His every hormone had been crying out for her since the first day he saw her sitting in that restaurant. That seemed like a lifetime ago. So much had happened since then. Now they were neighbors, landlord and tenant. Friends? That was the one relationship that he truly wished could thrive between them. Ironically, it was the one relationship he couldn't handle.

Of course his undying hope for setting the foundation for such a relationship was the main reason he'd asked her to join him that day. Inviting Capri instead of one of his many other friends would protect against mixed signals and waking up to a strange bedfellow the next morning.

At least that was his hope. Capri, however, was making that… well…hard, for lack of a better word. That dress of hers was certainly no help. While elegant and appropriate it was also chic and daring. The lovely cut of the frock was simply another form of torture.

"Tiberius, are you okay?" Capri couldn't help but ask when she noticed the drawn-tight look on his face yet again.

"How 'bout a drink?" He was patting her hand where it rested through the crook of his arm

Capri reciprocated with a hand pat of her own and nodded toward the group of older gentlemen waving at them. "Doctors?" she guessed.

"What else?" Tiberius decided to put off the much-needed drink for a bit more socializing. He squeezed Capri's hand, urging her to stop for a second. "I…um…I wanted to thank you for coming with me today."

"It was a pretty tough offer to refuse."

He remained serious. "Thank you anyway. Your company was very much appreciated."

Capri was silent, her mind going blank at the honesty she glimpsed in his words, in his light eyes. She simply nodded and managed a soft smile before they moved onward.

Later, as they swayed along the edge of the polished hardwood dance floor on the second-level balcony of the posh mansion, Capri rested her head against Tiberius's broad chest and let herself be lulled by the beat of his heart. She believed she could have danced against him forever. Even in the midst of a party, she felt as if they were in their own private escape with only the waving palms and a view of the Atlantic for company.

"You asleep?" Tiberius angled his head and tried to get a look at her face.

Capri nuzzled her head into his chest. "Not yet."

"Bored?"

"Not *even*." She looked up at him. "Thank you for bringing me with you. Today has been like a dream. The atmosphere, the food, even your colleagues have been fantastic."

A playful light gleamed in Tiberius's eyes. "You know Dr. Prentiss was staring at your chest from the time he started that stale conversation with you about slipped discs."

"I know." She laughed. "I think it's cute that a man his age still has an eye for the ladies."

"Cute, huh?" Tiberius nodded, his deep-set gaze scanning the crowd. "I'll remember that when I'm an eighty-two-year-old doctor."

"If you've got *half* his spunk, look me up."

The teasing moment gradually segued into something that hinted at being erotic. The fact was evident in Tiberius's gaze. He needed something to rid himself of the urge to damn the consequences and sample what he yearned for.

"Dr. Thomas's yacht." He tilted his head toward the cove where the vessel was docked. "Sometimes, he takes friends all the way out to Cuba." He nodded at the interest on Capri's face. "Word is, he worked on some huge political figures in his day."

"How huge?" Capri asked, her eyes wide. They grew wider still as Tiberius began to share.

* * *

Capri leaned against her front doorjamb and watched Tiberius as he called out for Droopey. They'd just returned from the party, and she'd promised coffee to take the chill off the evening, which had suddenly turned cool.

"Lewey's gone, too," she noted when Tiberius gave up his search and walked up to her door.

"She'll stick around when she comes back and sees the car in the yard," he decided while closing the front door behind him.

"I can't believe she's able to squeeze through those doggy doors." Capri headed for her kitchen. "Are they in all the houses you own?"

"Every one."

"Hmph, a serious dog lover." She chose a hazelnut blend and held it up for Tiberius's approval. When he waved his hand, she began to prepare the coffeepot. "Well I love 'em even though my *little* Lewey hasn't been all that little in ages."

"So how'd you get him?" He leaned back in the cream-cushioned, high-backed chair and watched her at the S-shaped counter.

"Lewey? Some kids were selling puppies on the street." She shrugged and smiled at the memory. "I looked at him and we chose each other. He was so tiny. The kids tried to get me to choose another, but I wanted Lewey. I knew he was a mixed breed but I didn't care about his pedigree until he gained fifteen pounds in two weeks."

Tiberius whistled.

Capri chose matching metallic-blue ceramic mugs from a small cabinet above the coffeepot. "I took him to a vet who was able to decipher the breeds. When he asked how big my house was, I knew I was in trouble."

Laughter filled the kitchen.

"So how'd you come by Droopey?" she asked while loading a wooden tray with cream and sugar.

Tiberius grinned, pulling the black suspenders from his shoulders as he remembered. "She was in one of the houses my grandmother left me. People just left her behind." A flash of anger tinged his words and face before he shook his head. "I saw her trying to hide in a corner. Small, terrified, and sad. *So sad…droopy.* I guess you could say she took my heart before I knew what hit me."

Capri didn't realize she was staring until Tiberius cleared his throat. "Sorry for keeping you in the kitchen," she said glancing across her shoulder. "This'll be done in a sec, but we can wait out front."

Silently, they headed out and were barely past the archway of the living room when Capri found herself in his arms.

"I thought you said—"

"Forget what I said."

Capri whimpered when his tongue thrust deeply and repeatedly inside her mouth. She let herself surrender to what had methodically invaded her thoughts over the last several weeks. Tiberius kept her there against the wall for what felt like hours. A brush of his hand sent the wispy straps of her dress falling past her shoulders and beckoned his attention to the bodice.

In one fluid motion, he lifted her and settled them both in the nearest armchair. Keeping her straddled across his massive frame, he buried his handsome face in the valley between her breasts and breathed in her scent.

Capri threw back her head when Tiberius tugged at the front of her gown and bared her to his gaze. His suckling on her nipples forced gasps and weak cries from her lips.

Tiberius relished the feel of the buds growing rigid against his tongue. His big hands roamed up her dress, pushing it higher to bare her legs and thighs. His fingers found their way to her panties. When Capri felt them curving into her, she gasped his name and fought against riding his nimble index and middle fingers.

"Tibe…Tibe, wait…Tibe…"

"I can't."

"Tibe, wait."

"Capri…" His forehead fell to her shoulder. "You're killing me."

"I want this, I swear I do," she admitted, her voice ragged with breathlessness.

A small furrow formed between Tiberius's sleek brows. "Then why—"

"I'm a virgin."

Tiberius pulled back as though he'd been burned.

"I thought you should know before…" She watched him blink incessantly. "It's not contagious."

Capri's attempt to lighten the mood didn't work. Tiberius was a picture of disbelief as his stare raked her face and body.

"You know, you *are* a doctor. You could see for yourself." Capri tried again to dispel the sudden tension between them.

Tiberius rolled his eyes. "Not funny."

Slowly, she pulled the bodice of her dress up. "I just thought you should know before we…"

He stood then with her in his arms and waited for her to slide down the length of his body. Capri watched as he awkwardly began to pat his pockets before extracting his keys.

"You're leaving?" she blurted.

"I…um…I should go find Droop." He gave her arm a quick squeeze, followed by an even quicker peck on the cheek and then he was gone.

Capri was greeted by a sloppy kiss when she opened her front door to get the paper the next morning.

"Where were you? Out all night without even a phone call," she admonished in a playful voice as Lewey simply nuzzled his massive head beneath her chin. She couldn't help but laugh, though her ease faded when she noticed Tiberius in his driveway. Her heart lifted when she saw him cross into her yard.

"Good morning."

"Hey." She stood watching Lewey race over to greet Tiberius.

"Capri, um, about last night. I'm sorry—"

"I shouldn't have told you."

"No, you should have." He weighed a set of keys against his palm and then slipped them into his trouser pocket. He shifted awkwardly.

"You're thinking differently about me now."

"It was just a surprise, Capri, that's all."

She tugged at the flowing cuffs of her gold chiffon robe. "You're having second thoughts now, though…about us being friends."

"Why would you think that?" His heart melted and inwardly he was wondering if he'd ever really wanted to be her friend. Still, he regretted that he'd given her that impression because of his own hang-ups.

Capri pressed her lips together and looked everywhere except his face. Tiberius had closed the distance between them and was cupping her chin. He kissed her forehead and then brushed his lips across her temple.

"How about we take the dogs somewhere this weekend?" he suggested, in hopes of putting a smile on her face. "We can make a real day out of it. Do you like to fish?"

The light reappeared in Capri's dark eyes. "I love it."

Tiberius shook his head. "Why am I not surprised? Saturday then? I'll pick you up at seven and we'll have breakfast somewhere first."

She nodded. "Okay."

Satisfied, Tiberius turned to snap his fingers at Lewey. "All right, playa!" he called and urged the dog inside the house with Capri before he left for work.

Chapter 9

Arriving at her office late the following Monday morning, Capri found a small white envelope lying on her desk. It was an invitation from Rod to attend the engagement party for him and Kiva. Of course, it came with specific instructions not to inform Kiva of the event.

"Oh well, at least someone's living the fantasy." Capri sighed, reading the invitation again. Gradually, her thoughts returned to the weekend spent with Tiberius and the dogs. Though they'd originally planned it as a one-day event, they had decided to make it a big production, and it had been fantastic.

Tiberius had arranged the weekend at a resort owned by a former patient. The place was a dazzling oasis hidden on a quiet stretch of beach far away from the energy of the city, and it seemed perfectly hidden from all outsiders. In spite of the clear attraction between Capri and Tiberius, they'd managed to enjoy a very platonic time, most of it spent enjoying the serene ocean views, food that was to die for, and walks along the remote beach. Conversation was plentiful and consisted of thoughts on careers and friends. Then there was the fishing. Marvelous fishing.

Clearly they'd both made silent decisions to keep the conversation and the mood free of anything erotic. Of course Droopey and Lewey helped with that greatly. The playful dogs kept their owners on their feet. By the time they returned home to prepare for another week of work, Capri actually believed a friendship between she and Tiberius might just be a possibility.

The soft yet insistent ringing of the phone interrupted her

thoughts. Lifting the receiver, she leaned back in her brown suede office chair. "This is Capri."

"Hi, it's Tiberius. Do you have a minute to talk?"

A quick shiver raced up Capri's spine when she heard Tiberius's soothing deep voice on the line. At the moment, however, she was more curious than aroused. "Yeah I have a few minutes."

"Did Rod send you an invitation to the engagement party yet?"

Frowning just slightly, Capri glanced at the card in her hand. "I'm looking at it right now, actually."

"Well, he sent me one, too, and I was wondering if you'd like to go together?"

Capri closed her eyes briefly and ordered herself to stay in control. It was only a party, she reminded herself. She and Tiberius had certainly enjoyed a party together before. It wasn't until the *after* party that things seemed to become a little too hot to handle.

"Capri?"

"Oh, I'm sorry Tiberius. Yes, I'd love to go with you."

Tiberius studied the phone after ending the call with Capri. Even as his mind screamed that attending an engagement party together was a beyond-stupid idea, he had continued the call and extended the invitation. Staying away from Capri was something he couldn't seem to do in spite of his best intentions.

At any rate, he needed something to brighten his day following yet another disappointing committee meeting regarding Alan Thomas's retirement trip down memory lane. He'd remained behind when the rest of the committee members had shuffled off and was beginning to work on his third drink when he noticed Rod shaking hands with his fellow lunch members. He was waving off the last two when he caught sight of Tiberius across the crowded dining room.

"You're looking happy," Tiberius noted once his friend had approached the table.

Rod's grin only broadened. "And you're looking just the opposite." He took the nearest empty seat.

Tiberius braced his elbows on the table and raked his fingers through his hair. "It's this retirement mess."

"Uh-huh. Well it sounds like you need somethin' to jazz it up," Rod noted once Tiberius explained what they had on tap. "It sounds stale."

"I know that much." Tiberius drained the rest of his beer.

Rod was tapping his fingers to his chin. "You've got a good start here, but it needs something to bring it home, give it zing."

"And what is that?"

"Well," Rod helped himself to one of Tiberius's untouched fries, "when *you* feel more excited about this thing than you do now, you'll know you've hit on it."

"Hmph. Thanks."

"So…what's really up?"

"Well, nothing to do with this, that's for damn sure." Tiberius didn't pretend to misunderstand his friend.

"Are you gonna make me guess?"

"Capri."

"Ah."

"Did you know she was a virgin?"

Rod smiled.

Tiberius seemed to deflate in his chair. "You knew and you didn't tell me?"

"Hell, man, why? Didn't you yourself say that messing around with your tenants was a bad idea?"

Pressing his forehead to his palm, Tiberius muttered something resembling a curse. "I wasn't expecting her," he confessed. "I thought I'd seen it all. I wasn't expecting her to surprise me."

Rod took another fry. "Yeah, isn't it funny how the good ones have a way of doing that?"

Tiberius sat tapping his fingers to the worn wooden dining table. "So, how'd you know she was…?"

"Kiva told me. She had to when she realized that every man I knew was asking me to set him up with Capri."

Tiberius didn't care for the sound of that, but he offered no argument. He buried his face in his hands and groaned. "This shouldn't have happened. I should've just rented her the damn house and kept my distance." He tugged on the sleeve of his navy blue suit coat and grimaced. "Now we're spending all this time together. Doing things with our dogs…" Still, he couldn't help but smile as thoughts from the weekend spent fishing replayed in his mind. The time had been easy and platonic, and he'd give anything to enjoy it again.

Rod was intrigued as he watched his oldest friend. He would never have expected to see a true ladies' man like Tiberius Montrae Evans so turned around by one woman.

"So what are you gonna do now? Ignore her?"

"No…I just asked her to come with me to your engagement party."

The resulting laughter turned many heads.

Pantsuits, evening gowns, shoes, wraps and other forms of clothing lay strewn all over Capri's large bedroom. She had rushed home right after work and headed straight to her closet to find something to wear for the engagement party. Amidst the motley crew of clothes lying against the azure satin comforter, Capri had narrowed her choice to seven outfits. She was trying to choose one, when the phone rang.

"Yeah?"

"So you're home already. I tried your cell but it went right to voice mail."

Capri pushed her hair behind her ear and dropped to her bed.

"Hey, Pep. Yeah, I think it's still deep down in my bag. We wrapped up the last session today, so I left early."

"What are you doing now?"

"Trying to choose an outfit to wear to Rod and Kiva's engagement party." Capri sighed.

Pepper sucked her teeth on the other end of the line. "I don't know why you sound so stressed, with all the outfits you have."

Capri ran her fingers over a short linen frock. "Well, I do have a date and—"

"Hold it. A date? You?"

"Yes, don't sound so surprised."

"But I am, dammit! Who is it? The good doctor again?"

"The good doctor," Capri confirmed.

"Well, I'll be damned. I'm glad to see you're finally coming out of your hermit stage, love."

Capri lay back on her bed and glared up at the ceiling. "I just hope I'm not making a mistake."

"Cappy, don't sell yourself so short. Maybe there's more to all this than you realize. Don't turn your back on it until you have all the facts."

"Well I might've talked to someone who does have the facts. A good number of them anyway."

"Who?"

"I don't know. I guess she was someone he used to see," she said, thinking of Clarissa.

"Mmm-hmm…she's probably a woman scorned and I suggest you not take what she said too seriously."

"You're right. I can't help but wonder though."

"Maybe she would have some facts based on her own experiences with Tiberius, but I don't think you can fairly compare what's going on between the two of you with whatever may have gone on between them. Maybe it's my own hormones talking but I suggest that you go out with him again and see if he's the jerk she claims he is or if she's trying to hold on to a dead relationship."

Capri still wasn't sure what to do. She did know that she loved Tiberius's company and really wanted to spend the evening with him. It was as simple as that. Or it could be. If only she knew.

Kiva sighed and tried to push away the braid that had escaped her high ponytail. Both her arms were filled with bags of groceries and she prayed she could make it to the kitchen counter.

"Where the hell have you been, girl?" Rod demanded to know as soon as he saw her walk through the door.

Kiva rolled her eyes and pushed one of the bags onto the counter using her hip. "Hmm…let's see—brown paper bags with food in them. You figure it out."

"Don't get smart," Rod ordered, coming up behind her to nuzzle her neck.

Kiva giggled and tilted her head to the side, allowing Rod's lips more room to roam along her smooth skin. "I went shopping and picked up a few movies we haven't seen."

"Mmm-hmm…"

"You don't sound too excited about spending a night at home with your girl," Kiva accused, pinning Rod with a hard stare.

Rod slid his hands around Kiva's tiny waist and pulled her close. "Maybe I'm tired of spending nights at home alone with my girl," he whispered with his mouth next to her ear.

Kiva pushed Rod away. "What's that supposed to mean?"

Instead of answering, Rod lifted Kiva into his arms and carried her out to the deck. He placed her on one of the lawn chairs and knelt before her. "Kiva…"

"What?" she quickly asked, unnerved by the serious expression she saw on his face.

Rod pressed a soft kiss against Kiva's bare thigh. "Marry me," he whispered.

Kiva's gasp sounded exceptionally loud in the peacefulness of the back yard. Closing her eyes briefly, she willed herself not to faint. "Rod...are you serious?"

Rod flashed a fantastic smile and shook his head slightly. "Baby, after four years, yeah I'm serious."

Screaming her joy, Kiva knelt beside Rod and threw her arms around his neck. "Yes, yes, yes..." she whispered, pressing dozens of kisses to his face. Laughing, the two of them collapsed to the deck and kissed deeply. Rod's hands disappeared beneath the fitted T-shirt Kiva wore, and caressed her back. Beneath the sun setting against the colorful late-evening skies, they were completely absorbed with one another.

"Kiva?"

"Hmm?"

"Baby, as much as I'm enjoying this," Rod began, closing his eyes again as Kiva tugged on his earlobe with her teeth, "and I *am* enjoying it, we don't have time."

"Why not?"

"We've got a party to go to."

"Oh really?" Kiva whispered, trailing kisses down Rod's chest as she unbuttoned the gray short-sleeved shirt he wore. When the tip of her tongue touched his navel, Rod's dark eyes fluttered closed.

"I guess this means we're gonna be late," he groaned.

At the same time, Capri was rushing to get home. She almost broke the speed limit trying to get there and cursed herself for getting caught in rush-hour traffic. The day at the studio had been one headache after another and she still hadn't finished everything. Sighing heavily, she glanced once more at her watch and wondered if she'd have the strength to enjoy the party. Of course, Capri knew she had to be there for Rod and Kiva. Plus she'd been anticipating her date with Tiberius all week. It had been several days since they'd seen each other and she was really looking forward to some time with him.

When she rolled up in her driveway, Capri didn't see Tiberius's truck in his yard. She breathed a sigh of relief, grabbed her purse, and hurried inside to shower and change.

A few minutes after Capri's front door slammed shut, Tiberius arrived home.

He cursed viciously for what seemed the twentieth time since he'd left the hospital. Today of all days, it appeared that all of his patients had gone into labor or had some sort of dire emergency requiring his attention.

Glancing at his wrist, he started loosening his tie and pulling off his suit coat. A grim smile marred his face as he shook his head and cursed his luck. Usually his professional life didn't affect his private one. Everything almost always fell into place so perfectly, he had plenty of time to socialize. Now, when he'd found someone he truly wanted to spend time with, he was unbelievably swamped.

The silent realization stopped Tiberius in his tracks. Lord, what was it about that woman? Sure he wanted her in his bed. She was vibrant, lovely and sexy as hell, but there was more. The fact that she was a virgin had stunned him at first, but it hadn't stifled his attraction for her. He wanted her more than ever and couldn't help but wonder how much he'd give to have her.

Clearing his head of that particular train of thought, Tiberius located his house key. "Droopey?" he called, glancing toward the backyard. "Droopey?" he called again, shrugging when the dog didn't appear. Going through the kitchen, he sat his briefcase on the counter and continued undressing as he headed upstairs to shower.

Capri had just donned her underwear when the doorbell rang. "Damn," she whispered, glancing at the clock on her nightstand and realizing that she'd taken much longer on her hair and makeup than she'd planned. Pulling a short gray silk robe over her lacy black garments, she ran downstairs.

Tiberius's unforgettable light eyes narrowed and he groaned deep in his chest when he saw Capri standing before him. Hoping she hadn't heard him, he cleared his throat. His eyes slid down from her curly hair, upswept into a French roll with loose tendrils dangling along her neck, to her beautiful round face before staring helplessly at her barely clothed body.

Capri, on the other hand, was so busy apologizing for not being ready, that she didn't notice the blatant male desire radiating from Tiberius's sexy stare. "It was so crazy at the studio today I couldn't get away on time," she rambled, even though Tiberius was hardly paying attention to her words. "Come on in," she invited, her dark eyes taking in the cut and fit of the long-sleeved olive-green shirt across his wide shoulders and muscled back. The linen shirt had a stylishly oversize collar and cuffed sleeves. The matching trousers molded to his lean waist and hips without appearing too snug. They hung loosely over his strong thighs and long legs, while showing just a hint of the considerable bulge between his legs.

Patting her hand against her chest, Capri cleared her throat and headed back upstairs. "I'm gonna finish getting dressed. Help yourself to anything," she called over her shoulder.

Tiberius clenched his large hands into fists and ordered himself not to take her offer the way he really wanted. He actually ached to touch her, and when she disappeared upstairs he headed to the kitchen for something cold to drink.

He was still there when Capri found him a few moments later.

"Are you okay?" she asked, concerned by the dazed look on his handsome face.

Tiberius ran on finger along the sleek dark line of his brows and closed his eyes. "Mmm-hmm…great," he grumbled, wishing the sight of her didn't affect him so. Unfortunately, the outfit she'd chosen for the evening would not allow that. The little black slip dress flared at mid-thigh. It had triple spaghetti straps that crossed over her back and allowed her to go braless. The front emphasized her exceptionally full breasts and small waist. When Capri finally walked away from him to check the back doors, Tiberius let out the breath he'd been unconsciously holding and poured another glass of lemonade.

"Lewey? Lewey?" Capri had ventured to the patio to call for her dog. When he didn't show, she shrugged and headed back in. "Looks like he's itching to get out of the house for a night. He's done this before so he should be fine."

"Droopey does the same thing sometimes," Tiberius said as he watched Capri lock the French doors leading to the patio. He waited for her to grab her wrap and purse, then escorted her out to his truck. Though his hand rested lightly against the small of her back, the touch still sent shivers down Capri's spine. Tiberius knew that she was just as affected by the closeness as he was, so he pulled his hand away.

When Capri settled into the passenger seat, Tiberius couldn't help but enjoy the way the strappy high-heeled sandals emphasized the shape of her legs. He ordered himself to focus on something else and slammed the vehicle's door shut with more force than necessary.

Chapter 10

The engagement party was held at a club that boasted a choice location right on the water. It was an old warehouse that had been converted into a stylish state-of-the-art facility. The main light source was the myriad electric candles on the walls and glass tables. Vintage disco balls hung from the ceiling, casting countless sparkles around the room. On the deck surrounding the building, moonlight reflected off the water and provided an even more exquisite source of lighting.

When Tiberius pulled to a halt in front of the club, Capri was speechless with surprise. Rod had said the party would be simple, but she should've known he'd go to the limit.

"Hold on," Tiberius called, when he saw Capri about to step out of the truck on her own.

Capri did as he asked and watched him get out of the car and walk around to her side. She admired his easy, unhurried stride, and the way his stylish attire molded to his large, athletic build.

Pulling her door open, Tiberius's deep-set gaze fell once more to her shapely legs and thighs. He offered his hand and smiled when she rested her slender fingers against his wide palm.

As they made their way into the club, Tiberius kept his hand around Capri's upper arm. His grip was light, yet vaguely possessive. Capri decided she was imagining the latter. Still, her lips parted slightly as she took several deep breaths to keep her cool.

"Champagne?" a waiter asked, holding out a tray of flutes filled to the brim with the sparkling liquid. Tiberius handed Capri a glass and took one for himself. Then they followed the waiter through the crowded club as he showed them to their table for the evening.

Tiberius and Capri had only been seated five minutes when people began stopping by to speak. Tiberius remained social, though he was more interested in watching Capri. He settled back in his seat, crossed his long legs at the ankles and simply enjoyed the sight of her. The way her dark eyes lit up and her smile dimpled held him entranced. Several people stopped to talk and Capri always seemed eager to hear what they had to say. She never appeared to be bothered or too tired to chat. If anything, she appeared even livelier with each visitor.

"Oh, isn't this nice?" Capri asked Tiberius later, when the waiter left with their dinner orders.

"Yeah, Rod went all out, didn't he?"

Capri nodded and looked around the club. "I'm so glad he finally proposed to Kiva."

"Yeah, I suppose I am, too."

Capri frowned and sent Tiberius a questioning look. "You don't sound very excited about it."

Tiberius shrugged and toyed with the thick black curls on his head. "It's just not a big thing to me, that's all. Marriage usually results in divorce, so I really never understood what the point was."

Capri was somewhat taken aback by Tiberius's cynical viewpoint and wanted to find out more. "Well, they don't always end up that way, Tibe."

"I didn't say they did, I said they *usually* did."

"I take it your parents are divorced?"

A muscle in Tiberius's jaw jumped fiercely. "You take it right."

Capri leaned across the table and patted his hand. "I'm sorry."

Tiberius's brown gaze settled to Capri's hand resting over his and he shrugged. "It's not a big deal, really. I mean, I spent much of my childhood wondering why they even bothered in the first place. Hell they weren't the only ones in my family who divorced.

I grew up around it, and that makes me not want to go through it with anybody."

"But you might not," Capri quietly pointed out. "Just because everybody else in your family split up, it doesn't mean the same thing will happen to you. What about your grandparents? They had a fantastic marriage, right?"

The look in Tiberius's warm brown eyes became cold and guarded. A humorless smirk crossed his mouth as he shook his head. "They were different, and I just prefer not to take the chance... ever."

Capri lowered her dark gaze to the table to hide the disappointment there. She didn't know what to do with the discovery and felt it best just to put it away from her for the time being. A part of her celebrated the fact that she hadn't fallen for him, but a more sensible part of her was forced to admit that she already had.

"Capri? Is that you, girl?"

"Well, hello." Capri smiled as Avery Erikson pressed a kiss to her cheek.

Avery leaned against a vacant chair at the table and pushed one hand into the pocket of his tan designer trousers. "I can't believe you took out enough time from that studio to come to a party."

"Well, he *is* my boss," Capri jokingly pointed out.

Avery laughed and noticed the large, intense-looking man also seated at the table. "What's up, man?" he asked, reaching over to shake hands.

Tiberius nodded and shook hands with Avery.

"Tiberius Evans, this is Avery Erikson." Capri supplied the introductions. "Avery's going to be the *face* for the new fragrance Bare Minimum." She ignored the humorous glint that flashed in Tiberius's eyes and turned to Avery. "Tiberius is an obstetrician and, I'm pleased to say, my new landlord," she explained.

"So, Capri, could I get you to share a dance with me?" Avery asked, glancing at Tiberius once the two men had nodded over each other's respective careers.

Capri looked over at Tiberius as well. Her lovely onyx eyes were wide in silent question.

Tiberius waved one hand lightly in the air. "It's okay," he assured her.

Avery led Capri out to the dance floor, but didn't take her too far from the table. Tiberius's pensive gaze followed every movement of Capri's small, sensual form. It was crystal clear that he wanted her. He settled on allowing Avery Erikson a few moments to enjoy having Capri in his arms. Of course, it wasn't long before he'd had enough of watching the twosome twirl around the dance floor.

He recalled their brief conversation about marriage and its results. He'd always felt his views for or against the institution were something to be admired. After all, the divorce rate was high enough without him added to the mix. But it might not turn out that way. Tiberius shook his head and recalled what Capri had said. He supposed anyone who had ever taken vows believed the same thing. His parents had at one time, at least he hoped they had. Grimacing at the thought, he tossed back the rest of his vodka tonic and pushed himself from his seat.

One thing was certain: Capri Timmons was far too special to wind up with someone who held such jaded views toward the institution of marriage. Because of his background, with the ugliness he'd witnessed between his parents, aunts, uncles...how could he believe that he was destined for a path that was anything different? Sure his grandparents had been happy, even blissful. Deep down, however, he'd always considered the success of their union a fluke—a beautiful fluke but a fluke nonetheless.

"Avery, what are you doing?" Capri's eyes widened slightly when Avery stopped swaying to the music. He was staring over her head, so she followed the line of his gaze and saw Tiberius standing behind them.

"You mind?" Tiberius asked Avery, who didn't argue about being cut in on.

Avery smiled down at Capri and then released his hold on her.

Tiberius slid his arms neatly around Capri's waist and held her firmly against him. Capri couldn't stop her gasp and stared up at him as her hands lay weakly against his chest.

In a world of their own, they took advantage of the chance to discover the feel of one another. Capri relaxed, rested her forehead against Tiberius's chest and inhaled his unique scent, enhanced by the cologne he wore. Her small hands smoothed over his muscular abdomen, before moving back up to knead his taut biceps.

Tiberius's hands weren't still, either. His fingers caressed Capri's bare back beneath the straps of her dress as his mouth caressed the soft hair along her temple. He didn't want to pressure her, but it was as though his hands had a will of their own. They lowered from the straps of her dress and down the small of her back to cup and briefly caress her buttocks. Capri lifted her head from Tiberius's shoulder, just as his lips slid down her temple to find her mouth.

The seductive atmosphere combined with the sensual crooning of Kem overhead provided added stimulus to what was happening between them. Erotic thoughts drew their body heats to a fevered pitch. When Tiberius thrust his tongue into the dark moist cavern of Capri's mouth, they both moaned. Capri's soft cries were smothered in the hot, wet kiss. Her fingers massaged the hard muscles in Tiberius's back as his tongue rubbed across her own. Capri's repeated gasps gave him more room to explore her mouth.

Tiberius grumbled something needy and incoherent. Capri wound her arms around his neck and the kiss deepened. The two of them almost forgot where they were, until clapping and shouting filled the room. Rod and Kiva had just arrived and everyone was crowding around them near the front of the club.

Capri pulled her mouth from Tiberius's and tried to push herself out of his arms.

"No," Tiberius whispered in a tortured, raspy voice. His embrace tightened around Capri's waist, as he pressed his face against her neck.

"Tibe...Rod and Kiva are here and we have to speak," Capri insisted, trying to catch her breath.

Tiberius held on to her a while longer, his chest heaving against hers as he took several deep gulps of air. Finally, he made himself let her go and they made their way through the crowd.

Kiva tugged on Rod's sleeve when she saw Tiberius and Capri walking toward them.

"You two came here together?" Rod blurted before anything else could be said.

Kiva pushed her elbow into his ribs. "What do you think?" she whispered.

Tiberius and Capri made a joint silent decision not to discuss it and pulled Rod and Kiva close for hugs. When the congratulations and best wishes were given, the engaged couple ventured out to the dance floor. Capri and Tiberius went back to their table.

Capri kept her eyes cast downward, unsure of what to say. Tiberius watched her for a while before moving into a seat next to her. He trailed a finger down the satiny-smooth line of her cheek and beneath her chin. Nudging her head up, he waited for her eyes to meet his before he spoke.

"I'm sorry if I just did something I shouldn't have, but...oh never mind, I—I'm just sorry."

The softly voiced admission caused Capri's heart to flutter madly, but she otherwise remained calm. "No, you didn't do anything wrong Tibe. There's nothing to apologize for. What's a little kiss between neighbors?" she said lightly.

Silently, Tiberius thanked her for that, though his narrowed gaze widened slightly. Clearing his throat, he reached for a fresh drink and took a long swallow. "Your honesty continues to surprise me."

Capri shrugged and let her eyes settle on Tiberius's wide, sensual mouth. "It's all a person really has," she intimated.

The electricity crackling between them was undeniable. They would've kissed again but their food arrived. Suddenly famished, Capri dug into the delicious shrimp fettuccine alfredo, unable to believe how hungry she was. Tiberius concentrated on his chicken cacciatore and silence settled.

It wasn't long before Rod and Kiva arrived at the table they were sharing with Capri and Tiberius. Laughter and conversation returned with the arrival of the happy couple and the celebration really began.

After the party ended about three hours later, Tiberius took Capri home. The ride was quiet except for the jazz vibrating from the stereo speakers.

When Tiberius shut off the silver Navigator's purring engine, Capri silently prayed that he would go home and let the evening end there. Of course he didn't, choosing to help her from his truck and follow her to her house. Capri didn't make a fuss but decided that once they were inside she'd make it clear that perhaps they should leave things at the friends-and-neighbors level.

No sooner had Tiberius slammed the front door shut behind them than he grabbed Capri's wrist and pull her to him. He was kissing her before any words could be spoken.

Capri would've slipped right to the floor beneath the erotic mastery of the kiss, but Tiberius didn't give her the chance. Determined to continue what they'd started at the club, he lifted her high against him and increased the pressure of the kiss. The last thing on Capri's mind was resisting. Threading her fingers through Tiberius's silky crop of hair, she was focused on returning the kiss with equal passion.

Tiberius let his hands mold to Capri's form like an artist creating a clay sculpture. He memorized every dip and curve time and time again. His large palms cupped her bottom before sliding around her thighs and silently ordering her to wrap her legs around his back. Capri complied and didn't realize they were headed to the sofa until she felt the thick cushions beneath her back. Tiberius ended the kiss and trailed his moist lips down the silky column of her neck. He pressed his tongue against the base of her throat while one hand sought her breast. Capri pushed her head farther back into the cushions and cried out so softly she was barely heard.

Tiberius massaged the soft, ample mound of her breast before easing the straps of her dress across her shoulder. He raised his head and watched as he tugged the bodice across one voluptuous breast. Groaning, his eyes narrowed and he took the firm nipple between his lips.

Capri had never experienced such intense pleasure, and she was in a state of exquisite delight. Unconsciously, she arched her back, pushing herself closer to the sensuous tugs of Tiberius's lips. Capri was so enthralled by what was happening she instinctively stroked the bulge in front of Tiberius's trousers.

Tiberius circled his tongue around the nipple that rose to a hard nub beneath his merciless tugging. A knowing smile crossed his lips when he heard Capri cry out. Having wanted her for so long, he couldn't keep his satisfaction quiet, either.

"I want you in my bed so much I can't think," he whispered raggedly against her ear.

The words, though alluring and passionate, doused Capri's passion. The full scope of what was happening—what was at stake—brought her out of her dream state.

Tiberius tuned into the tension of her body, and he looked down at her. A curious frown darkened his handsome face as he put his weight on his elbows. "What is it? Is everything all right?"

"Could you just let me up?" Capri whispered, nudging her hips against his.

Confusion and unease continued to mar Tiberius's light eyes as he did as she'd asked.

Capri took a deep breath and kept her cool. "I guess it's my turn to apologize." She laughed uneasily as the thought settled.

Tiberius pushed one hand though his hair. "What happened? What is it?"

Capri rolled her eyes toward the ceiling, not wanting to look at him. "Look, Tiberius, I have lived with this decision for a long time. I've ruined what could've been several nice relationships because I couldn't change my mind and go back on it."

Tiberius was frustrated but tried to articulate his feelings as best as he could. "And you don't think I understand that?"

"Many men can't."

"All right then. Since you're being honest I guess I can as well. For a long time I've looked at sex as…just sex. Not love, and certainly not a path to marriage." His words were fueled by sheer frustration and anger toward his own jaded psyche.

Capri could understand how he must feel. All she wanted was to make love to him, but she knew getting carried away in sensations and pleasure could be dangerous. "I guess Clarissa was right," she breathed and waited for her words to click.

Tiberius blinked and dipped his head closer to Capri. "What are you talking about?"

Capri eased off the sofa and brought her hands to her sides. "I met her coming from your house one day a while back. The two of you had been arguing."

"And?"

Massaging the tight muscles in her neck, Capri sighed and walked away. "It's nothing… I… She tried to warn me about you."

Tiberius's laugh was short and relayed his intense disgust. "And you believed her?"

Capri kept her back turned and didn't answer. "Not at first, but if what you just told me is your way of thinking when you're involved with a woman, then it's no wonder she…"

Tiberius pushed himself off the sofa. Shoving his hands into his trouser pockets, he asked, "Yeah, it's no wonder she what?"

Capri turned around to face him, her large dark eyes sparkling with understanding. "Can you really say that you don't think that way anymore? You've got to be true to yourself, Tibe. If you can't, then it's just like you once said—there are gonna be a lot of misunderstandings and drama and ugly consequences. We've been pretty good friends." She smiled. "We've been *damn* good friends, and that's something I never thought would be possible. Giving in to this, we just may lose that friendship and I don't want that to happen. Do you?"

A look of pure surprise flashed in the beautiful depths of Tiberius's eyes. He blinked and looked as though he were torn. Yes, he treasured the friendship they were crafting. Unfortunately, his steadily building romantic desire for her would not be quelled. He nodded anyway and let his gaze travel down the length of her body. "No, I don't want to lose that, either," he said right before he turned and left the house.

Later that evening, Capri was still mulling over her conversation with Tiberius. In spite of all she'd said about the importance of a healthy friendship, alone, she admitted it was all a load of bunk. She was telling him to be true to himself when she couldn't even do the same. Only to herself could she confess that he was what she really wanted. Pushing the coffee mug she held back into the cabinet, Capri groaned and leaned back wearily against the countertop. She was frustrated, confused, and growing increasingly frightened by the disintegration of her most cherished personal decision. Glaring at the wall phone, she chose to share her concerns with those who'd always given her the sagest advice.

* * *

"If we could get back to the subject at hand?" Capri urged through the laughter still claiming her. She'd managed to get her three older sisters on the line for a conference call. It had taken a bit of persistence since Cassandra lived in Phoenix, Cannon out in Oregon, and Carla in Atlanta, but thankfully the sisters never passed on the chance for a venting session.

"Cap, you're gonna have to forgive us for acting so silly. I guess we're just trying to soften you up."

Capri shook her head. "Thanks, Carla, but I'm afraid you've got your work cut out for you there."

"Honey, I think Carla means that you're not gonna like what we're about to tell you," Cassandra explained.

"What?" Capri's ease was starting to dwindle.

Cannon sighed over the line. "Sweetie, I'm actually the only one who *saved* herself for marriage."

Silence filled all four lines for a while until Cassandra spoke up.

"Carla and I...indulged," she shared, and uttered a quiet laugh. "Carla at least comes in second with marrying the man she gave her virginity to, while I..."

"Why didn't you guys tell me?"

"Mama," they all spoke at once.

"As far as she was concerned, Cannon's shining example was the *only* example and she dared us to tell you any different," Carla said.

"With you being so much younger than us, talks about our sex lives weren't typical conversation," Cannon said. "There was never a real reason or opportunity for you to be told any different."

"Capri? Is this about you trying to live up to something you don't even believe in or want?" Cassandra asked.

"Hmm, well I didn't realize that I didn't believe in it or want it until recently."

Carla chuckled. "Sounds like someone's being tempted."

Capri closed her eyes. "Guilty. And I've been criticizing myself all over the place, calling myself a fool for falling for some tall, caramel-toned doctor with curly hair and deep eyes." Capri grimaced when she heard the sighs of appreciation follow her description. "There's more to him y'all, lots more."

"Mmm," Carla's laughter was just below the surface, "and you want *lots more* from him, too, don't you?"

Silence.

"Oh, Cap, there's nothin' wrong with that," Cassandra cried. "You *are* free to change your mind, you know?"

"That's right, Capri," Cannon chimed in. "Just because this decision was right for me doesn't mean it's right for you. There are no rules here, no *proper* ways of doing things, and there's absolutely no one waiting to brand you with a scarlet letter because of it."

"So what's stopping you, girl?"

Capri laughed over Carla's question. "Me, of course." She sighed.

The phone rang the next morning, just as Tiberius set a plate filled with fluffy scrambled eggs on the table. Wiping his hands on the dish towel hanging on the refrigerator, he picked up on the third ring.

"Yeah?"

"Tibe? Did I catch you on your way out?"

"Kiva? No I was just getting ready to eat breakfast. What's going on?"

Kiva took a moment to answer. "Well, um, I wanted to know if I could stop by and talk to you today?"

Tibe pulled at the hem of the orange Florida Gators T-shirt that fit snugly across his wide chest. "Sure, Kiva, any time. It'll have to be at the hospital though 'cause I have a full load today. If you want to stop by around two, I should be there."

"That's perfect. I'll be there."

Tiberius turned and leaned against the brick kitchen island. "So, you wanna tell me what's going on or what?"

"Well, Tibe, if you don't mind, I'll just wait 'til I see you."

Tiberius shrugged. "Fine with me. See you later." He stared at the phone for a moment once the connection had been broken. Then, he replaced it on the base connected to the side of the island. Picking up the tall glass of orange juice he had sitting on the counter, Tiberius walked over to the window and enjoyed the view of his backyard.

The serene expression on his handsome face slowly changed to a murderous frown. Taking a closer look out the window, his temper went though the roof. "Capri Timmons!" he yelled in a thunderous tone that nearly rattled the windows.

Chapter 11

"Lewey! Lewey, come on now. I'm starting to get worried!" Capri was standing on her front porch with her hands on her hips. She hadn't seen her dog since the prior afternoon.

Sighing, Capri smoothed her hands over her shorts and was about to head back inside the house. Just then, Lewey ambled around the side of the house, his soft whining catching Capri's attention.

"Oh, where have you been, you bad boy," she chastised, kneeling to hug the mammoth animal.

Lewey propped his heavy head on Capri's shoulder and nipped at the flimsy tie of her yellow halter top. He rested there for only a moment, making a mad dash to the back when he heard a roaring voice coming closer to the house.

"Capri!"

Frowning, Capri pushed a curly tendril of hair behind her ear and stood. Her eyes widened slightly when she saw Tiberius storm around the corner. "Tibe, what—" She tilted her head, noticing the fury on his face. "What happened?"

In response, Tiberius motioned for Capri to follow him back to his house. He ignored her questions and led her through the gate and alongside the wooden fence.

"Tibe? What's going on?" Capri asked as she noticed they were walking straight toward the backyard. "Where are we going?"

Tiberius made no attempt to answer and simply continued his trek along the fence. When he finally reached his destination, he pointed to what appeared to be a huge tunnel dug beneath the fence.

"Well?" he roared.

Capri shrugged. "What?"

"Do you see what your dog did to my fence?"

Capri wasn't intimidated by the expression on Tiberius's face. If anything, she became just as furious. "You're accusing Lewey of this? How do you know it was him?"

Tiberius rolled his eyes toward the sky. "Please, girl, from the time he smelled Droopey he planned a way to get over here!"

"Oh, please! Why couldn't it be Droopey trying to get in my yard to Lewey?"

A devious, humorless smirk added a sinister gleam to Tiberius's handsome face. "Well, according to you, it's us males that have sex on the brain all the time, not the other way around."

Capri's full lips pushed into a pout and she stood shaking her head at Tiberius. "This is really unfair. All the other dogs out here and you pick on mine."

"I've never had problems with the other dogs out here. They're from top breeders and are well-behaved."

Capri's arched brows drew together and she took a step closer to Tiberius. "What are you trying to say?"

Tiberius stepped closer as well. "I'm saying that if that mutt has gotten Droopey pregnant—"

"Mutt?"

"Damn right. I don't want her having a bunch of half-breeds."

"You are ridiculous!"

"Yeah, well you'll see how ridiculous I am when I dump all the runts on your front step."

The two of them stood there arguing like children for a few more moments. Soon Capri was so furious she couldn't see straight. Raising her hand, she brought a halt to the conversation.

"Listen, Tibe, why don't you go somewhere and find Droopey? Tell her I said I hope she had fun."

Tiberius kicked his fence and then watched Capri switch away. His eyes were trained on the white shorts that revealed just a hint of her bottom. Not wanting her to arouse any more emotions in him, he squeezed his eyes shut. It didn't work. After a moment, a smile crossed his lips and he shook his head.

Although he'd sworn it would never happen, he'd let a woman get inside his head. Capri Timmons, with her baby-doll looks, had captivated him both physically and mentally and there was no doubt about it.

Pushing his hands into the deep pockets of his saggy blue jeans, Tiberius walked back to the house. For a moment, he wondered how it had happened. How had he allowed this woman to slip past the wall he'd painstakingly built around his emotions? True, she was vibrant, beautiful and voluptuous, but so were many of the women he knew. No, it was Capri's sometimes seductive, sometimes innocent, always alluring persona that had done it. For the first time in his life, he found himself wanting a woman as more than a lover. Tiberius finally realized that he actually wanted a woman to talk to and be with platonically as well as sexually. Sadly though, it was that unsatisfied sexual aspect that was causing him to act like such a jerk at the moment.

Laughing at himself now, Tiberius told himself to forget it. Capri already had a negative view of him, and it was obvious that she wanted to keep it.

"Damn," he cursed his luck. The time when it mattered most that a woman find him irresistible and she wanted nothing to do with him.

Capri decided to spend the day at home, even though she had several things to finish at the studio. Unfortunately, between the engagement party, the fight with Tiberius that morning and their bittersweet conversation the night before, and the revealing talk with her sisters, she felt completely worn down.

Although she could still kick Tiberius for being such a jerk about the incident with the fence, Capri knew what had happened after the party was her fault. Well, maybe *fault* wasn't quite the right word to use there. However, she was the one who had begun the conversation. She'd pushed Tiberius away and said what she did knowing he'd be discouraged…and put off. What was happening between the two of them had felt so sweet, so perfect.

She replayed the conversation with her sisters for the umpteenth time and knew that, if anything, the talk had convinced her that there was no right or wrong decision. Regardless of the choice, Capri was certain that sex was something to be shared between two people who cared and knew enough about one another to cherish the act when it happened.

Of course, their conversation had given her some pretty keen insights to Tiberius. Clearly his perceptions of love and commitment had been set at a pretty early age. It had to have been tough watching every important relationship surrounding him fail. The love affair between his grandparents was probably viewed by him as unrealistic, unattainable, a fluke. It was sad really, and until Tiberius was ready to risk his heart, he'd never know what kind of relationship he was capable of handling. Moreover, neither would she, she mused.

As if on cue, Lewey came sniffing around. He seemed somewhat uneasy and probably suspected Capri was angry. He kept his distance, staring at her with huge sad eyes.

"Come 'ere," Capri called, tugging on the big leather collar around his neck. "Do you have any ideas on the subject?" she asked Lewey. A sad expression clouded her lovely face as she thought about how nice things could be with Tiberius. He was smart, successful, considerate and undeniably handsome. It could've been so nice.

The phone began to ring and Capri moved away from Lewey. She buried her face in her hands and took a deep breath before answering.

"Hello?"

"Hello, what's got you sounding so sad?"

Capri smiled and leaned back in the armchair. "Hey, Avery."

"So what's wrong?" he persisted.

"Nothing, I've just got a lot on my mind."

"Well, it sounds like you need to get out."

"Avery—"

"Now wait a minute. I know you probably weren't planning on calling me. Even though I went as far as giving you one of the cards I reserve for the best people—"

Capri interrupted with a chuckle.

"But," Avery continued, "I decided to give it one last try."

"Well, I admire your determination."

"Does that mean you'll go out with me?"

Why not? Capri thought to herself. Avery seemed like a nice guy. Besides, the shoot was done and they no longer had a working relationship. Plus, she had to do something to get Tiberius off her mind. "I suppose I won't be breaking any rules by saying yes, would I?"

Avery chuckled. "You won't break a one."

Capri chewed her bottom lip for a second and then smiled. "All right, when and where?"

"So, I'll see you and John next week?"

Christina Wilkes sighed and nodded at her doctor. "He'll be here even if I have to bring his office with me."

Tiberius laughed and led Christina to the elevators. "Well do your best, but don't forget he's working hard to support these twins."

"Oh, I'll keep that in mind when I feel like breaking his arms because he works too much."

"Thanks," Tiberius said through his laughter.

The elevator finally arrived and Christina stepped inside just as Kiva stepped out. Tiberius waved his patient off, and then turned to Kiva.

"Hey, you," Tiberius greeted, kissing his best friend's fiancée on the cheek.

"What's going on with you and Capri?" Kiva asked, immediately after they hugged.

Tiberius sighed and took Kiva's hand. "Let's talk in my office."

"I'm sorry, Tibe, I just want to know," Kiva said when the office door shut behind them.

Tiberius pulled off his jacket and threw it on the suede sofa near the bookshelf in a far corner. "No offense, Kiva, but why are you so interested?"

Kiva fiddled with one of her braids, but kept her brown eyes on Tiberius. "I just don't want to see her hurt."

"Why the hell are you and Rod so protective of her? She's a grown woman, you know?"

"We both think of her like a little sister."

Tiberius rolled his eyes and walked behind his desk. "Well, I think you should let it go," he mumbled.

"Not a chance," Kiva replied hotly. "Just in case you forgot, Tibe, I know how successful you are at getting women into bed."

"Excuse me?"

Kiva didn't let Tiberius's voice intimidate her. "Do you recall any of my girlfriends that you've dated in the past?"

Tiberius prayed he wouldn't lose his temper. "So?"

"The ones that you've been intimate with and the ones that you've dumped?"

Tiberius raised his hand and stood. "All right, Kiva, hold it, because what you're talking about has nothing to do with you."

Kiva raised her hands as well. "Okay, I'm sorry. You're right and I'm sorry. I just don't want to see Capri hurt."

"My God, you and Rod are really terrified that she could actually become involved with me," Tiberius said, his intense brown eyes narrowed in enlightenment.

Kiva lowered her gaze to the floor. "It's not like that."

Tiberius shook his head and turned to stare out the windows of his corner office. "It doesn't matter anyway. She's figured me out."

The weary chord in Tiberius's deep voice caught Kiva's. "What do you mean?"

Tiberius turned and leaned against the window. He decided to confide in Kiva. "After the party we went back to her place. Things got intense. She was into it as much as I was."

Kiva took a seat in one of the chairs facing Tiberius's desk. "What happened?"

Tiberius shrugged one shoulder and ran his hand through his hair. "At first I wasn't too sure, but suffice it to say that she doesn't believe I'm ready to accept the kind of relationship she wants. She does however love our *friendship*. She doesn't want us to lose that." He grew serious. "Funny thing is, I don't want to lose it either. Bottom line is she thinks I'm as shallow as a bathtub and she's probably right."

"Did she say that?"

"She should have. The crazy thing is that it was probably the one time that it wasn't completely true."

"Really?" Kiva asked with intrigue.

"Really. I mean Kiva, I'm not gonna lie to you. I know what kind of man I am when it comes to women and I want Capri. I *want* her so much that half the time I can't even think straight. Last night though, I think I realized that I wanted more than the obvious."

"I can't believe it," Kiva whispered.

"Yeah, well, I'm getting a lot of that lately," Tiberius grumbled, hurt by Kiva's comment.

"Sweetie, are you serious about this? Because it sounds like you want a relationship with her and...well...it's just not you."

"Don't get excited. I'm not a completely changed man."

Kiva shook her head. "Tibe, you've had a lot of women in your life and they've gone as quickly as they've come. Now, Capri is in the picture and suddenly you're at least considering a real relationship with a woman? It's quite a change. Are you sure it's not just physical attraction talking?"

"No. No I'm not sure, but I know that's not all of it," he said, before throwing his hands up in defeat. "Hell, what difference does it make? I might as well forget it. I don't think Capri trusts me as far as she can throw me."

Kiva pushed herself from the chair in front of the desk and walked over to Tiberius. "Listen, um… Lord, I don't believe I'm saying this… Look, just don't give up on her yet."

Tiberius frowned and looked down at her. "What's that supposed to mean?"

Kiva hesitated a moment before speaking. "Don't give up on her. Don't give up on yourself."

Later that afternoon, Tiberius was out in his backyard. A black scowl was on his face as he looked down at the hole tunneled beneath the fence. He'd been debating since he'd gotten home on whether to fill it.

"It'll probably be a waste of time," he grumbled, looking up when he saw Capri come out on her patio with Lewey. In her arms she carried a huge bag of dry dog food.

Tiberius watched the comical scene for a moment. Lewey was practically knocking Capri's tiny form aside as he tried to catch the food in his mouth before it could reach the bowl. When Lewey realized Capri was tougher than he thought, he waited for her to finish.

Tiberius slowly headed along the fence closer to Capri's patio. He waited until she finished feeding her dog before he said anything.

"Do you mind coming over here for a second?"

Capri looked across the fence at Tiberius and gave him a

suspicious glare. After a moment, she stepped off the patio and came closer to the fence.

"I was gonna grill some steaks later. Do you wanna come over?"

Capri studied the look in Tiberius's warm brown eyes and wondered if he was trying to make up for their argument. It was hard to resist him when he watched her with such innocence on his gorgeous face.

"Tonight's not really good for me."

He ran one hand through his hair and looked down at the ground. "Listen, Capri, I'm not gonna try anything. I just wanted us to have dinner together."

Capri curled her small hands over the fence posts and shook her head. "It's not that."

"Well, have dinner with me then." He spoke softly, trying to persuade her.

"I can't."

"Why?"

"Tibe…"

"I'm listening."

"I have a date," she said, looking him straight in the eye.

Obviously surprised, Tiberius gave a short laugh and looked away. "Oh," was all he managed to say, due to the fact that his heart was lodged in his throat.

"That's why I'm feeding Lewey out back. He'll be there until I get home," she rambled, feeling the need to explain.

Tiberius raised his hands and backed away from the fence. "I'm sorry, I didn't mean to push."

"That's okay," Capri whispered, feeling as let down as Tiberius looked.

Tiberius pushed both hands into the pocket on the front of his lightweight University of Miami sweatshirt. He flashed Capri his dimpled smile. "Well, have fun."

Capri inched away from the fence as well. "Thanks."

Tiberius's gaze narrowed as he watched her leave. After a second, he realized he'd clenched his hands into a fist which he then pounded against his thigh.

Capri didn't want things to be awkward between her and Tiberius, and hoped that extending an invite to the wrap party of the fragrance shoot might settle the tensions that had risen between them. Unfortunately, this get-together wasn't the prim, well-mannered affair they'd attended for Dr. Alan Thomas. This time around, sex was an almost tangible guest amongst the bevy of scantily-clad women and the men all vying for the chance to take one of them home.

Tiberius was trying his best to have a good time, but all he really wanted was some alone time with Capri. He knew he wouldn't survive into the third hour of the party and prayed Capri wouldn't give him grief for wanting to leave soon. *Very soon,* he thought, watching the clown who had been trying to get a moment alone with Capri several times that evening.

Tossing down the rest of his bourbon, Tiberius watched Capri across the room laughing and dancing with Avery Erikson. How ironic was it that sex was usually the only thing on his mind with a woman? Now, with Capri, sex was the one thing he *didn't* want to think about. And watching her take a twirl with the slick model on the dance floor certainly wasn't helping.

"I just want you to know that you're really bruising my ego here. I've asked you out three times and each time you cancel out on me," Avery said.

Capri tilted her head and frowned. "Are you forgetting our date not too long ago?"

This time, it was Avery's turn to frown. "No offense, but that wasn't exactly what I had in mind. Meeting in a noisy sports bar for drinks—and to make matters worse, we wind up running into people from your studio."

Capri shrugged. "I thought we had a great time."

"Downing beers, popcorn and pretzels while debating baseball isn't my preferred method of dating." He gave her hand a tug. "What I'm envisioning is us sharing a bottle, or three, of very expensive wine in the privacy of my very expensive condo."

She nodded. "I see where you're coming from, and I appreciate you being so great about it, but I'm just going through some things right now and I'd be terrible company. Trust me."

"Do you think you'll ever take me up on my offer?" Avery asked smoothly, giving her a wink.

"It's hard to say. Things are pretty…turned around right now."

"Well, you know where I am when you change your mind, right?"

Capri gave him a playful glare. "Right."

Avery gave her a light squeeze. "We could stop somewhere for a drink or something, maybe talk a little more after the party."

Capri thought for a moment. "Well I came here with someone so I'm afraid tonight's not good."

Avery clutched his heart. "You really know how to hurt a guy, Ms. Timmons."

Capri laughed and winced. "Sorry."

Avery stroked his smooth jaw and stared off in the distance. "Just promise you'll make it up to me soon. I really want to get to know you better. The fact that you're a photographer threw me for a loop. It captivates me, you know? All that braininess wrapped in such a pretty package." His dark gaze was unreadable. "I've got to know more," he said.

Capri snapped her fingers. "That might be pretty tough if we get another photo-spread assignment."

Avery clapped a hand to his forehead and uttered a pained sound.

With his mind set, Tiberius stood and up checked his pockets for keys before heading to the dance floor. "Time to go."

"Hey!" Avery blurted, as Capri was easily extracted from his embrace.

"Tibe, what—"

"Hey, man," Avery interrupted before Capri could finish. Avery realized he wouldn't *finish* either, as the look stemming from Tiberius's eyes warned him that he wouldn't care for the response.

Capri noticed the look too and absently patted the front of Avery's shirt. "It's all right. I promised we wouldn't stay long anyway." She turned and smiled at Avery. "It's fine. We'll talk soon, okay?"

They drove back in utter silence, not even the radio playing. Capri wasn't sure whether to be stressed or flattered by Tiberius's obvious jealousy. When they finally pulled into her driveway she left the truck without waiting for Tiberius to open her door and began walking herself to the door.

Tiberius caught up to her easily, snaking an arm about her waist and helping to escort her for the rest of the short walk. Coolly, he selected her house key from the chain while she strained against him. Inside, he tossed the keys to the message table, slammed the front door shut and pulled her smack against his chest.

Capri opened her mouth to blast him and was hindered by a searing hot kiss. Tiberius's tongue burrowed deep into her mouth hungry lunges that would've snapped her head back had she not met the force with a fire of her own. Straining to get away from him was no longer an issue. Instead, she strained to get closer, loving the soft animal growls that vibrated in his throat as the kiss lengthened. By the time he was done, her panties were soaked with need. Her head swam so that all she could do was cling to him for support.

"You were right about me and that's the *only* thing on my mind when I think about you." He was eerily calm. "It's the only thing I think of when you're near me. I don't think I'll have another damn thing on my mind until you're in my bed. I don't want to be your friend, not half as much as I want to be your lover. I was willing to try being friends as opposed to dealing with all the *drama* that would rise if one of us got the wrong idea. But I guess I was the one who got the wrong idea." At last sparks of unease clouded his eyes. "I thought I could do this, Capri, but I can't, and it's just time that I stopped pissin' around and told you the truth."

The lost look in her eyes shredded his heart, but he left without looking back.

Capri lost track of time once Tiberius had gone. He'd taken her by complete surprise with his confession. She tried to collect herself and was just about to let Lewey back into the house when the doorbell rang.

She hesitated, not sure if she was praying for or dreading Tiberius's return. Squaring her shoulders, she went to answer the ring.

"Avery?"

"I came to check on you," he said, and stepped boldly across the threshold. "I didn't like the way you left with your friend." He glimpsed cautiously around the living room for any sign of Tiberius.

"He's long gone." Capri smoothed her hands across the front of her mauve tube dress.

"Ugly scene?"

"A surprising one, but it's over. I'm sorry." She cleared her mind with a quick shake of her head. "Come on in."

"Thanks," Avery said as he strolled into the room.

"So how'd you know where I live?" Capri inquired while draping her jacket across the back of an armchair. It was then that she noticed Avery held her purse.

"You left it at your table back at the party," he explained.

"God." Capri sighed as she took a seat on the sofa. "Thank you so much." She hadn't even thought about her purse, or anything else for that matter, in hours. "So, um…how was the rest of the party?" She was determined not to let her thoughts bring her down again that night.

Avery grinned and clued her in about the rest of the get-together which had grown more outrageous as the evening progressed.

"Well, at least the clients were happy," Capri laughed.

"They certainly were." Avery was sitting on the opposite sofa, his elbows resting on his knees as he watched her closely. "I made no secret of the fact that I'd like more work in this area, and since they love you it could be a possibility."

Capri shrugged. "I don't see why not. Besides, it'll keep you closer to your family," she offered as she recalled his sick aunt.

"Not really, since they all live out west."

"Listen, I've got coffee. Would you like some?" she offered with an inviting smile. She was a little too foggy-headed and just plain agitated to call him out on his lie.

Avery followed Capri into the kitchen and watched her at the counter before closing the distance between them. Slowly his fingertips brushed her bare arms before curving across her shoulders.

"You're tense," he noted, working his thumbs in slow soothing circles at the base of her neck.

Capri tapped the side of the coffeemaker. "This'll help."

"I can think of something better."

But Avery's strokes were only a blaring reminder that he wasn't Tiberius, and it was Tiberius that she wanted. She turned to let Avery down easily, but she never had the chance.

Before she could say anything, he grabbed her shoulders and pressed his mouth to her neck. The mug on the edge of the counter shattered on the floor as they brushed against it. Capri's obvious attempts to push Avery away only motivated his attempts to get closer. Heart pounding with fear and anger, she shrieked. The sound, combined with the breaking mug, woke Lewey from his slumber on the patio. He was on his feet immediately, barking and growling outside the sliding-glass doors.

Avery was no longer the compassionate, considerate acquaintance. He was the direct opposite. His hands were everywhere. He pushed Capri's dress higher and squeezed her buttocks tightly. Capri's terrified screams were loud and piercing, but she fought back and gave him everything she had. Still, Avery was totally oblivious to the heavy blows that landed on his neck and back.

Hauling her tiny frame against his larger one, Avery rushed over to the dining-room table and pushed everything off it. He held Capri there and moved between her legs. Lowering his mouth to her ear, he kissed the lobe. "Don't worry, after this you won't be so uptight."

"What the hell is wrong with that mutt?" Tiberius grumbled, glancing across the yard at Lewey. The dog was jumping around the double glass doors and barking ferociously.

It took a moment, but Tiberius thought he heard something else. Something that sounded like a scream. His mind was instantly alert and he whirled around. He cocked his head for a second only before he went tearing over to Capri's house.

Nothing mattered from that point on except getting inside that house. Tiberius knew he'd never make it through the glass doors, so he went around front. He truly feared his heart would explode, it raced so fast as Capri's screams grew louder.

"I'm coming," he yelled, glancing briefly at the Porsche in the driveway. Grimacing, he wouldn't allow himself to dwell on who it belonged to or why they were there. Leaning his shoulder against the front door, he braced himself, and then put all his strength into it.

The wood splintered immediately beneath the force, and Tiberius crashed through. His brown eyes instantly landed on Capri in the dining room. When he saw her cursing and struggling on the table beneath another man, he froze.

Another terrified scream from Capri snapped him out of his trance. He bolted across the room and in one swift movement he pulled Avery Erikson off Capri. Tiberius was more furious than he'd ever been as he threw Avery into a wall and watched as he slid to the floor.

"Capri?" Tiberius called, as he stared at Avery. When she didn't answer him, he turned. "Capri?"

"Hmm? What?" she jerkily replied, her eyes snapping to Tiberius's face.

"Call the police," he requested, not wanting to take his eyes off of Avery.

Capri was about to move, but the sound of sirens caught her ears. "I think that's been taken care of."

"Here, take this, too," Tiberius grumbled, tossing Avery's suit coat to a nearby officer. The police had taken statements from both Tiberius and Capri. Avery had regained consciousness in time to be escorted into a waiting police car.

Tiberius watched from the front porch as Avery's shiny Porsche was towed away. "Can I get you some more tea?"

Capri shook her head against Tiberius's chest.

Tiberius squeezed her shoulder and led her back inside. Capri dropped to the sofa and leaned back against Lewey, who was lying on it.

"Are you okay?" Tiberius asked, kneeling before her and patting her knee.

"I'm fine," Capri assured him, though her usually melodic voice was eerily hollow and toneless. "Tiberius, I haven't had a chance to thank you for getting here before Avery…"

"Shh…" Tiberius soothed, rubbing her knee.

"Reason number one for leaving the city," Capri blurted, her anger surfacing.

The deep dimples appeared in Tiberius's cheeks when he smiled. "Honey, I'm afraid that bastards like that are everywhere."

Capri gave a solemn nod. "I know that. Guess I actually thought it'd be different here."

Tiberius knew what she was trying to say. Before he could get another word out, though, Capri stood and walked away.

"Tiberius, I think I need to be by myself now, if you don't mind."

"You might need me for something."

Capri smiled. She didn't want to appear cold after all he'd just done for her, but she couldn't face him or anyone just then. "You're right next door. If I need anything, I'll call you."

"You promise?"

"I promise."

The last thing Tiberius wanted to do was leave Capri alone, especially not that night. Of course, he knew that more than anything she didn't need to be pressured and decided to leave her be.

Chapter 12

There were charges to be filed and Capri was determined to see Avery Erikson pay for what he'd done. She spent the next day away from work after welcoming the morning by berating herself for being so naive. Being attacked like that had been such a real possibility when she'd lived in the city that she felt silly for thinking a move would change things. She'd learned the hard way that she was wrong.

Of course, work could not be ignored. The next day found Capri brushing off her woes and strolling into the studio offices bright and early.

"All right, all right break, it up!"

Kiva stopped nibbling on Rod's ear and quickly turned toward the door. A big smile brightened her lovely dark face when she saw Capri. "Girl, what are you doing back so soon!?"

"That's what I want to know," Rod asked, standing when Kiva moved off his lap to go hug Capri. "I thought I told you to stay home a few days?"

Capri held on to Kiva and nodded at Rod. "You did, but I'd go crazy staying there all day."

"So go lay on the beach or something," Rod said, pulling her close. "How are you doing?"

Capri relished the tight hug, before stepping back. Her thick curls bounced around her face as she tossed her head back. "I'm fine. It could've been a lot worse."

Rod's slanted dark eyes narrowed even more. "We know. Tiberius told us about most of it. We didn't come over because he said you needed to be alone."

"He was right," Capri confirmed, toying with the silver-tone zipper on her coral knit suit. "I'm glad he was there when I needed him, though. I'll never be able to repay him."

"I don't think he's expecting that. Tiberius is a great guy," Kiva firmly stated when silence settled over the room.

Rod and Capri frowned and sent Kiva the strangest look. They both knew she wasn't one of the doctor's biggest fans.

Still, Capri couldn't argue. "Yeah…he really is," she agreed, before clasping her hands and giving Rod a pleading look. "If it's okay I'm going to put in a half day."

Rod waved his hand. "You don't have to ask me that."

The three friends embraced briefly before Capri said her goodbyes and left. When the door shut behind her, Rod turned to his fiancée.

"Tibe is a great guy? What made you say such a thing?"

Kiva pursed her lips and gave Rod a sour look. "I never said he was a monster. I just didn't think he was the type of guy a woman like Capri would want to think about having a serious relationship with."

Rod sat on the edge of his desk and crossed his arms over his chest. "So what happened to change your mind?"

"I happen to know he cares a lot about her."

"And how do you know that?"

"He told me."

"Ha! And you believed him?"

Kiva shrugged. "Yeah, but it wasn't easy. You know Tibe is the first one to tell a person how much he hates serious relationships. I think that maybe Capri is changing that for him. I also think that he's scared to death about it. It's not easy for a man like Tibe to walk away from that player lifestyle."

Rod gave her a sly smile. "So you've decided to help him out?"

"Well, I don't know what I'm doing. I do know that I'm gonna stop discouraging Capri from giving him a chance. I think he may really be serious about her."

"What do you have in mind?"

Kiva pushed her hands into the front pockets of her long, beige linen skirt and sighed. "I'm going to give Capri a few more days, and then we'll invite them over for dinner."

A look of feigned surprise came over Rod's handsome dark face. "*We're* inviting them?"

"Mmm-hmm. I just hope Capri'll come over when she finds out that Tiberius will be there."

Rod shrugged. "So don't tell her."

Kiva smiled. Walking over to Rod, she slid her arms around his neck. "Mmm…great minds think alike."

After work, Capri had decided to spend the remainder of the afternoon lounging on her cozy patio. She tried to concentrate on the book in her hands, but kept glancing toward Tiberius's house. Tossing the book to the edge of the lounge, Capri closed her eyes and leaned back. After a moment of silence, the phone rang. She stared at the small, gray cordless for a moment before reaching to grab it off the table a few feet away from her.

After the fourth ring, Tiberius knew he should've hung up, but he kept the phone pressed to his ear. He hadn't seen Capri in several days and knew he at least needed to hear her voice. His heavy brow wrinkled as a dark frown clouded his face. "Where is she?" he grumbled.

"Hello?"

Tiberius had just pulled the phone away from his ear when he heard the soft voice on the other end. "Capri?"

"Tibe?"

"Yeah…I was just about to give up on you."

Capri closed her eyes and imagined him standing before her.

After so many days of not seeing Tiberius or talking to him, a phone call was a welcome treat.

"You okay?" Tiberius asked, his voice sounding soft, but concerned.

"Yeah, I'm fine. Just getting a little rest."

"I'm sorry, was I disturbing you?"

"No, no, I'm glad you called."

"You are?"

Capri hesitated, before nodding. "Yes."

Tiberius grinned and leaned back in his office chair. Capri would never know how much her tiny admission meant to him. "So, did you go in today?" he asked, not wanting to scare her away by making the conversation too intimate.

"I showed up for a half day. Rod let me have the rest of the afternoon off."

"You sure you're okay?"

"Positive."

"Have you, um…heard anything about Avery?"

"Well, my lawyer and I think we're getting the run-around and I've got the feeling the bastard's slimed his way out of this kind of thing before."

Tiberius grimaced. "Well a mess like this can drag on for a while, especially when a quote-unquote *celebrity* is involved."

Capri sighed and pushed her curls out of her face. "I know that. I just want to make sure that he has an attempted rape conviction on his record. I don't want it swept under the rug like it never happened."

"Good for you," Tiberius encouraged, though discussing Avery Erikson was triggering his anger. "Look, can we drop this subject?"

Capri laughed. "Fine with me."

"I'm here if you ever need to talk about it, though."

"Thank you. And I need to apologize for the way I acted that night. I shouldn't have pushed you away after you helped me."

"After what you'd just been through? Please, I assure you I understand."

"No, you don't."

"Meaning?"

Capri shook her head. "Listen, it's a long story."

"I've got time."

The rich, deep tone of Tiberius's voice sent such pleasurable sensations down Capri's spine she could've talked to him all night. "You know, Tibe, I really don't want to waste the little time we have talking on something so heavy, all right?"

"Fine, but I hope you won't keep me guessing too long."

"I promise I won't," Capri told him, feeling as though they were talking about two different things.

The rest of the conversation was soothing and calm. In spite of all the hurtful words and misunderstandings Capri and Tiberius talked like old friends, neither of them wanting to hang up.

"She's here."

"How does she look?"

"Tibe won't be able to keep his eyes off her."

Satisfied, Kiva nodded and turned back to the mirror to finish the elaborate coiffure she was creating. As promised, she'd waited a few evenings before inviting Capri and Tiberius over for dinner.

"You sure about this, Kiva?" Rod asked, brushing invisible lint from the collarless charcoal sport coat he wore.

"It's just dinner, baby."

"True. But you're messing in a situation that has nothing to do with you."

Kiva sighed and leaned against the dresser. "Like I said, it's just dinner. Now I know I've been real hard on Tibe in the past, so this is my way of making that up."

"And what about Capri?"

Kiva rolled her eyes and checked the backs of her diamond studs. "Please, Rod, I've seen how she looks at him. She's trying to protect herself, but it's still obvious that she's very interested in him."

Rod stepped closer to his fiancée and slid his large hands around her waist. "I just hope this amateur attempt at matchmaking won't blow up in your face."

Kiva closed her eyes and relished the feel of Rod's hands roaming over the light, airy material of her dark-chocolate slip dress. "I don't think there's a chance of that happening."

"Thanks again for inviting me over," Capri said, as she accepted a glass of wine from Rod. "It's been a while since we've gotten together for dinner."

"I know that's what I was telling Rod," Kiva called from the kitchen, winking at her fiancé when she saw him.

Capri took a deep breath and ventured down the short hall that led to the dining room. The elegant room was on the side of the house overlooking the ocean. It was encased in glass and gave a spectacular view day or night. Capri took a sip of her drink and soaked in the relaxing atmosphere. The soft jazz from the built-in speakers made her want to pull up a chair and stare out into the night.

Turning away from the arched doorway of the dining room, Capri took a moment to admire the table. The fine china, shining silverware and delicate crystal added even more beauty to the already dazzling room. Suddenly, though, a frown wiped the easy look off her face and she quickly headed back to the kitchen.

"Kiva? Why is the table set for four?"

"Um…" Kiva glanced over at Rod who shrugged. "Well, uh…I always set an extra place."

Capri toyed with the thin gold chain around her neck and nodded.

She turned to head out of the room, and then whirled around again. "You guys didn't invite Tiberius for dinner, too, did you?"

Rod and Kiva exchanged glances and were speechless. That, however, was enough for Capri. She set her glass on the kitchen table and saluted them.

"Good night," she said.

"Capri, wait!" Kiva called as she and Rod rushed out of the room.

Capri raised her hand. "Listen, you two, I appreciate what you're doing, but I've thought about it and there's no future in it, so why bother?"

"You can give him a chance."

Capri gave Kiva a solemn smile. "There's no reason to. Good night." She left Rod and Kiva staring after her as she grabbed her purse and walked toward the foyer. When she pulled open the door, she slammed right into Tiberius.

"Whoa," Tiberius exclaimed, his big hands immediately settling around Capri's hips.

Capri looked way up into the intense brown depths of Tiberius's eyes and tried to balance herself. "Sorry."

"No problem," he softly assured her, letting his hands drop so she could step back. His warm gaze swept her tiny form encased in a sleek, black halter jumpsuit. The neckline dipped low to give an unforgettable view. The suit molded to her curves and flared into a slight boot leg showing off her black platform mules. Tiberius took his time enjoying the sight before him, and then gave her a funny look. "Um…Kiva didn't tell me you would be here. Have y'all already eaten?" He glanced at his watch.

Capri shook her head, her curly bob bouncing around her face. "Uh—no. Kiva was just finishing up."

"Oh. So where are you going?" he asked, walking inside and making her move away from the door.

Capri's doelike gaze was wide. She watched him push one hand into the pocket of the stylish black trousers he wore with a matching long-sleeved collarless shirt. As he stood there waiting for an answer, she was at a loss for words.

A knowing smile brought to life the dimples in Tiberius's cheeks. In a smooth gesture, he softly patted Capri's shoulder, moving her farther into the foyer. Before anything could be said between them, Rod and Kiva were out front.

"Tibe! I'm so glad you got here!" Kiva sighed in relief as Rod shook hands with his friend. "Is everything okay, Capri?"

Choosing not to make a scene, Capri nodded and walked back into the house. She missed the triumphant smile Kiva sent to Rod.

Kiva's dinner was a smorgasbord of heavenly dishes. There was roasted chicken, juicy and seasoned to perfection. There was also a cheesy macaroni casserole, delicious steamed broccoli with a light butter sauce, steamed cabbage, fluffy cornbread, and a crisp garden salad topped with a creamy light dressing.

Everyone filled their plates several times and ate heartily. When Kiva mentioned dessert, no one knew if they had room.

"So, Kiva, I guess you and Rod won't be registering for any china?" Capri asked, sipping from her wineglass as she eyed the impressive array of china on the table.

"No, we're most definitely registering for it. All this is old stuff our parents gave us."

"But everything looks so new," Capri noted.

A bright smile pulled at Kiva's full mouth. "Hey, I don't care. I'm trying to get as many gifts as I can. I don't plan on doing this but once."

Everybody laughed, but Capri couldn't help but glance at Tiberius. She would've loved to ask him if he thought Rod and Kiva's marriage would last.

Kiva noticed Capri looking at Tiberius and tapped her fingers in front of Rod's plate. "Baby, would you help me with dessert?"

Rod's slanted black gaze narrowed and he gave her a strange look. "It's only pie."

"Well I need your help with the knife," Kiva said, grabbing Rod's hand and pulling him along behind her.

Tiberius drank the last bit of wine from his glass and looked over at Capri. She was looking down at the table and twiddling her thumbs.

"You know, we live right next door to each other and I see Rod and Kiva more than you."

Capri's head snapped up when she heard Tiberius speak. She smiled. "Yeah, it's like our schedules are total opposites."

Tiberius chuckled and propped one finger alongside his temple. "That's for sure. At least we've got the phone. I still prefer to see how you're doing in person, though."

"Oh? Why is that?"

Tiberius gave her a sneaky smirk. "So I can see if you're being honest or just telling me what you think I wanted to hear the other night."

Capri nodded, then leaned back in her chair and spread her arms. "So was I just telling you what I thought you wanted to hear?"

Tiberius leaned close and propped his chin on his fist. "Hell, no, you look very good," he whispered, his deep voice slightly raspy.

Laughing softly, Capri shook her head. "It hasn't been that long."

Shrugging his large shoulders, Tiberius leaned back. "It doesn't matter anyway. You always look gorgeous."

"Thank you." Capri's heart was doing crazy flips at the soft-spoken way he complimented her. She tilted her head. "Tibe? Are *you* all right?"

The question took him by surprise and he took a moment to answer. "Me? I'm fine." But he really wanted to tell her what he'd said the night they had their fight was wrong. That maybe he had been wrong all along. Would she believe him? For that matter, would *he?*

"Tibe?" Capri called, resting her hand across his.

Before he could answer, Rod and Kiva came back into the dining room.

Chapter 13

Capri was in her office going over proof sheets when Rod knocked and walked in. They spent a few minutes on some small talk, which Rod was terrible at. Still, with all that had taken place over the last few weeks, including the very public and very successful court proceedings against Avery Erikson, there was quite a bit to chat about.

"So now are you going to tell me why you're really here? What's *really* up?" she asked when Rod finally took a breath.

"The Haize Fragrance people want to cancel Avery's spots."

Capri tossed the magnifying glass she held to the desk and flopped back in her chair.

"They're dead set against having him in any of the ads."

"I'm not surprised. Hell, I don't blame them." Capri rubbed her fingers through her curls. "Doesn't mean I have to like their decision though, does it?" Suddenly all the weeks spent dealing with the greasy Don Juan seemed even more aggravating.

"So what now?"

Rod leaned forward to brace his elbows on his knees.

Capri winced. "What? Are they going with another studio?"

Unexpectedly, Rod's expression brightened. "Actually, they love your work and your style…they want to keep the same flavor but with a different face."

"Well, they saw our stock before they settled on Avery, and even with him we were fishing outside of our pool."

"Think maybe we can latch on to the same magic again?"

Capri was running through a mental list of faces in her mind, and she didn't know if it was a blessing or a curse that she continued to come back to the same face over and over again. "Tiberius."

Rod couldn't have been more stunned. "Tibe? Tiberius Evans? God…you know…that may not be such a bad idea. He's got a fresh face. A good face."

"Excellent body."

Rod shivered. "Okay, this conversation is getting just a little too weird for me."

"What's weird about it? We do this all the time, almost every day."

"That may be true but I'm usually not talking about someone I've known since the diaper stage." He shook his head as Capri laughed. "Let me know what he says when you ask him."

Her laughter stopped. "Rod, I—"

"He won't do it if I ask him. I couldn't ask him about this anyway since I'd be too busy laughing. Which means that it's up to you. And since this was all your idea…"

Capri wouldn't waste time with more arguing and decided there was no time like the present. "I'll have Tandy call the Haize people," she referred to her assistant. "And I'll go talk to our *face*."

Rod grinned. "Good luck."

Capri was hoping she'd be asked to wait when she arrived at Tiberius's office. That would've at least given her a bit more time to prepare. There he was, however, right when she arrived. Perched on the corner of his assistant's desk, Tiberius fidgeted with an electronic calendar. His brow was furrowed in concentration and Capri was struck.

"Good afternoon," the woman behind the desk was saying.

In spite of the polite and chipper greeting, Capri found that she could only raise her hand slowly in response. She had already caught Tiberius's gaze.

"Can we talk?" she asked, when he stood up from the desk and raked his stare across her face and body.

Absently, he tossed his BlackBerry to the desk and waved her forward. "Hold my calls, Pam."

Capri took a minute to admire Tiberius's office which was like an extension of his home—comfortable and spacious. The walls were filled with photos of people she presumed were new parents with bundles of joy just delivered to them by the good Doctor Evans. When the door closed behind her, she braced herself and faced him.

"I can't believe I've never seen your office before."

He shrugged slowly. "Time flies."

"Right." Capri nodded.

"Are you all right?" Tiberius was asking, already moving across the room to tower over her.

Capri felt her throat dry as she looked up at him. "I'm, um…" She finished off with a nod. "I need to ask you something. It's a favor. A big one."

It was on the tip of his tongue to say that he'd do anything she asked, but something told him to hold off on saying yes just yet. Intrigued, he put more distance between them and leaned against a far wall. "Shoot."

The word brought a smile to Capri's face. "Actually, that's exactly what I want to do. The fragrance people pulled the ads with Avery. They want a new face and they want it now." She took a breath. "We want yours."

Tiberius was just beginning to smile over the fact that the saccharine-sweet gigolo had lost his gig. Then he realized what Capri was asking.

"Mine. *Mine?* No."

"Tibe—"

"Sorry Capri. I—I, um…" He laughed. "No way."

"Now, just a minute." Capri rushed over, grabbing his hand and pushing him to the arm of the sofa in the office. "Just hear me out for a second. You'd be great at this."

He snorted.

"Trust me. Rod thinks so, too."

Tiberius laughed.

"And I haven't even told you about the trip. It's a long weekend in the Keys. We'd leave Thursday and be back on Tuesday."

"Capri, I can take a long weekend to the Keys anytime I want."

"Then do it for me." She laid her hands flat on his chest and pleaded with her eyes.

"You'd ask me to do this even after the things I said to you?"

Capri didn't need to be reminded. "Please, Tibe?"

"Nothing's changed," he warned, brushing his fingers against the zipper tab that secured her lavender top. "I may not be as much of an idiot as Avery was. I definitely understand that no means no, but I want you and you know that. Will you be able to get this thing done with that kind of tension?"

She'd have to, because finding someone more perfect and in such short working time would be next to impossible. She was desperate.

"So you'll do it?"

He brushed the back of his hand across her jaw and shrugged. "When do we leave?"

Chapter 14

The crew trickled in at various points the following Thursday. The plush villa rented by Haize Fragrances was right on the water and would be home to them for the duration of the shoot. Most of the sessions would take place in and around the area as well.

For such a spur-of-the-moment deal, Capri thought they'd done remarkably well. She and Tiberius had taken separate cars to the Keys and hadn't seen each other until early that morning during breakfast. Clearly the female models were more than pleased with Avery's substitution. The four leggy beauties had practically avoided Avery at all costs outside of the photo sessions. His replacement, however, warranted 'round-the-clock attention, it seemed.

Capri found a model seated on either side of Tiberius when she arrived in the lovely sun-drenched dining room that morning. Laughing at every remark he made, the models behaved as though they were riveted by all the talk about his profession.

She took stock of the women fawning over Tiberius. The models, both molasses-dark and flawless, would contrast well against his caramel coloring. The women were both tall and striking. Capri wondered if Tiberius's profession lent to his nonplussed demeanor around the goddesses. He treated them politely and with a fair amount of charm, still, he didn't come across as though he was awed or in bliss over having his ego so thoroughly stroked by their interest. The manner in which he struck her then had Capri both captivated and impressed.

"It all sounds so fascinating, but I could never tolerate all that school for so long." Alaina Farmer cringed as the idea filled her head.

Stacia Harold seemed to agree. "I don't know, Al. It might not be so bad with a study partner like Tiberius."

This time it was Capri who cringed.

Tiberius noticed and took a quick swallow of his coffee to hide his smile.

"More coffee, Tiberius?" Molly Dendrix offered a dazzling smile as she took his cup.

Capri rolled her eyes when Denise Shepard took Tiberius's plate and filled it with another hearty helping of bacon and eggs.

"All right everyone, let's gets serious here," Capri called the group to attention once everyone had had their fill of the catered meal.

"We'll begin with the shoot this evening. Wardrobe left Miami this morning. It seems there were some last-minute alterations needed to accommodate our new model."

A round of chuckles filled the room. Capri shook her head when the women all gazed at Tiberius adoringly.

"We're hoping for beach shots around sunset, and, as we all know, that's the busiest time down here." She massaged her neck while drawing a frowning face on the pad where she'd noted the shoot. "We've managed to have a portion of the beach sectioned off for the shoots so let's pray for no hiccups." She closed the pad portfolio and smiled refreshingly. "With that said, I'll see you all this afternoon. Please make this your last meal of the day until after the shoot."

Everyone stood to set off for their respective tasks. Capri was about to leave when she thought of one last thing to jot down in her notebook.

"Do you need me?"

Her head whipped up at Tiberius's question, and for a second or three she had no idea how to answer.

"Just make sure to protect your face." She smirked when he

grinned. "Be back here by three. I've got some prep work to do with the crew, scouting other locales and such." She glanced past his shoulder. "Guess you can enjoy your day. I don't think you'll be lonely for company."

Tiberius glanced back at the four models waiting at the archway of the dining room. Turning back to Capri, he gently tugged a lock of her hair and then walked away.

Evenings in the Keys were breathtaking, to say the very least. Capri thanked the awesome heavens above for their beauty and proximity. She might actually pull this off. All the players were in their places and looking sharp. No matter her agitation over the giggling models earlier that day, they did their jobs very well. The four lovelies complemented their devastating honey-toned counterpart to a tee.

The group met before sunset on their stretch of beach and began with preliminary shots and other requirements. By sunset, the shoot was well underway and concluded just as the sun bade farewell to the beach.

"Good job, kid! You ever do this before?"

Tiberius waved off the lighting engineer's raves. "Never before and never again," he told Randy Morgan.

"He's right, man, not bad," Zeke Bozman confirmed his boss's comment.

"You put most of the models we've worked with to a stinkin' shame."

"Hell, yeah, you're better than most who've spent their entire lives doing this mess."

Tiberius shook his head at Kade Adams's and Henry Owen's comments and watched as they packed up their equipment. "If I'd ever known I'd be *this* good at it I'd have tried long ago and found another way to pay for med school."

Laughter roared along the dusky beach and Tiberius was easing out of the tailored slate-colored suit coat when his photo partners cornered him.

"Just one drink, Tibe?"

"To celebrate your first shoot?"

"Please?"

"We know the best spots down here."

Of that, Tiberius had no doubt. Still, he would've much preferred spending the evening with Capri. He asked the models to excuse him as he headed off to find her. While he knew she'd probably decline any offer to spend time together he wanted to ask just the same.

Capri meant far more to him than he'd led her to believe. She meant more to him than he himself had realized. But what good would come of it? The fact that she was saving herself pretty much meant marriage was her wish with the right man. Was *he* the right man? How could he be when every relationship he'd seen involving the most important people in his life had failed? Where did that leave him?

He watched her at the tables where the photo equipment was being stored. She looked pretty involved with the lenses she was switching out. And besides, the girls were calling out to him again, asking him to reconsider going out for drinks. Cowardice won out. With one last look at Capri, he left for more lighthearted enjoyment.

Capri noticed him leaving and didn't know if it was relief or frustration that made her sigh. Tiberius had warned her that the weekend would be tense, and although they'd barely spoken two words to each other, things were definitely strained.

Just do the job, Cap. Keep your mind on the work and off of... everything else. But seeing as how Dr. Tiberius Evans *was* the work, she accepted the fact that this was a no-win situation.

* * *

Whatever tensions existed, the group focused and persevered, reaching their goal of completing the task at hand. Everyone worked diligently to meet the deadlines, braving tourists, a short stint of uncooperative weather, and their own personal dilemmas. The job soon reached its end. On the last night of the shoot Capri gave the fancy caterers their walking papers and ordered in all the trimmings for a memorable barbecue. It went over exceptionally well and helped to work off all the frustrations the deadline-driven job had set in motion.

Following a perfectly grilled rib eye, a loaded baked potato, and some buttery rolls, Capri took her third bottle of Red Stripe to the balcony for a little alone time.

Everyone else was still going strong—eating, drinking, playing. Capri was sitting on a lounge chair happy for the solitude. She felt her eyelids grow deliciously heavy while she enjoyed the smells in the air and the waves roaring in the distance. Time passed in a lovely haze, so much so that when her eyes fluttered open it took her some time to get her bearings.

Tiberius stood across the balcony; a bottle of Heineken in one hand and a look of unease on his face. "You mind a little company out here?" he asked.

"Not a bit." Capri waved her hands toward the view. "I don't think I could get away with keeping all this to myself anyway."

Grinning, Tiberius strolled closer to the lounge area.

"Too much for you in there?" Capri noted.

"I haven't partied like that since college."

"Stop," Capri ordered, her dark eyes wide as she feigned surprise. "I could've sworn someone told me you were this big-time playboy?" Her gaze was riveted on his bare chest as he shrugged.

Tiberius swigged back a little more beer. "I prefer to play under less chaotic circumstances…like a restaurant where you can sit and talk and actually *hear* the other person."

Capri laughed, but it wasn't long before the tensions between them brought a serious tone into the mix.

"I'm sorry, Capri. What I said that night…I'm sorry." He rubbed fingers through his dark curls while stepping closer. "I, um…I was trying to be honest, but I never should have been cruel."

Capri fumbled with the wispy front ties of her bikini top. "The truth often hurts." She sighed.

"But you didn't deserve *the truth* like that."

"Do you still feel that way?"

"I'd be lying if I said I didn't."

Capri met his gaze then. "So would I."

Tiberius blinked, the glint in his light eyes confirming his surprise over her admission. He studied her closely for a moment and then set aside the bottle and joined her on the chair she occupied.

They were kissing madly in under a minute. Tiberius's hands were everywhere, and he vaguely noted that she wasn't stopping him. His tongue delved deeper each time it thrust past her lips and rough groans filled his throat when she met his kiss with her own brand of fire.

The coral bikini top offered little in the way of confinement and Tibe lost himself in the feel of her alluring endowments. Holding one satiny mound in his hand, he weighed it, delighted in its firm yet giving texture and brushed his thumb across her nipple until he felt the tip firm in response.

Capri savored it all. When his mouth lowered from her breasts to trail her body, she simply arched into the kiss. The wispy white cotton skirt she wore covered a bikini bottom which provided little protection against Tibe's searching tongue. She cried out, unmindful of who might be looking or listening. She'd dreamed of being touched that way but had never allowed herself to be. Instinctively, her hands lost themselves in Tiberius's glorious hair once his head was burrowed between her thighs. Her entire body trembled when his lips nipped at her womanhood. The delight he offered only urged her to ride on his experienced tongue.

Her soft moans and breathless calls of his name simply fueled his confidence and need. He was painfully aroused and knew she was the only one who could soothe the ache. He pushed those thoughts to the back of his mind and focused on pleasuring her.

And he did that quite well, if the orgasmic shrieks she began to utter were any clue. Tiberius felt even more ravenous for her taste and relentlessly drove his tongue inside her as she climaxed. He groaned when her desire flooded his tongue, and he drank in her essence as her shudders subsided to quivers.

Capri yearned for his kiss when he rose over her once more. Her lashes fluttered in stunned amazement at the taste of her body on his tongue. She was so depleted that she fell asleep when he cuddled her close. Sleep didn't visit Tiberius for quite a while.

Capri and Tiberius headed home in their respective cars on Tuesday. They took different routes, but arrived home within minutes of each other.

Tiberius was unpacking his truck when Capri pulled up in her driveway. A resigned smile curved her mouth as she exited her Pathfinder and slowly walked around front to Tiberius's house.

"Can we talk?" she called across the yard.

Tiberius asked no questions and simply waved a hand toward his home. Capri crossed the driveway to follow him into his house.

"Let's go in the living room," Tiberius said, laying his hand on the small of her back.

Capri stood in the middle of the darkly furnished, elegant room. Tiberius stopped a few feet in front of her and pushed his hands into his pockets and waited.

"I've been feeling like a real fool lately," Capri admitted. "Especially after what happened with Avery."

Tiberius's expression lit with realization. "I hope you're not blaming yourself for that."

"I'm not blaming myself for what he did, but I do take a certain responsibility for not seeing what was right in front of my face."

"Sounds like blame to me."

"Just let me say this, all right?" Capri raised her hands. "I've spent a lot of time complaining about men and their ulterior motives, and then I couldn't even gauge the intentions of one whose motives were clearly plastered all over him. Avery had already started to piss me off the first day I met him and I think I let some of that fuel my suspicions about you."

"You had every right to feel that way about me. Especially after what I told you," Tiberius offered.

"What I didn't tell you was that I wanted more than a friendship, too, and that it terrified me," Capri confessed. "If you don't know by now how bad I want you in my bed, then you're blind."

"Capri—"

"Can I finish please?"

Tiberius pressed his lips together and took a seat on the cushiony sofa.

"I've asked you to be honest and I have to do the same. I've been having doubts. Doubts about my decision to abstain. Not knowing if it's what I really want, and coming to grips with that is almost stifling."

"Capri, you should know that I'm determined to have you in my life. Simple as that."

"It's not that simple, Tibe. You don't know what you're saying."

"Why? Because you're a virgin?" Tiberius snapped, becoming frustrated by her resistance. "Is that why you're so against getting close to me or letting me get close to you?"

Capri winced slightly at the words, and knew she had no choice but to stop beating around the bush. Smoothing her hands over her thighs, she stood up and walked around the sofa. "It's an issue, and don't act like it isn't. The decision to save myself for marriage is a big deal for me."

Tiberius closed his eyes and shook his head. "So you don't trust me?"

"I trust you believe what you're saying."

Tiberius's frown changed into a stunned look and his long, heavy brows lifted a few notches above his eyes. He sank to the armchair nearest him, as his intense gaze traveled over Capri's voluptuous form. "You're so sure it could never happen for us the way you want?"

Capri smiled. "The way I want? As it stands, you'd have to ask me to marry you."

Tiberius looked as though he wanted to say something, but didn't know what. Capri sent him a sympathetic look over her raised hand. "You don't have to reply to that one."

Clearing her throat, she grabbed her purse off the sofa and walked toward the living room doorway. Passing the armchair where Tiberius sat, she gave his shoulder a soft squeeze. "Good night, Tiberius."

Tiberius, however, wasn't about to let her go so easily. Surprising her, he grabbed her wrist and guided her until she was in his lap.

"Don't leave yet," he whispered against her parted lips before sliding his tongue deep inside her mouth. His hands roamed the length of her legs, stopping at the junction of her thighs where he rubbed the pad of his thumb against her femininity. He broke the kiss and caressed the smooth line of her neck, before settling to the cleft of her breasts. He groaned as his tongue traced the visible curve of one mound.

Capri uttered a weak, needy sound and threaded her fingers in Tiberius's soft hair. She cupped the side of his face and urged his head up. Losing herself in their embrace, she pressed her mouth against his and kissed him deeply.

"I know we can work this out," Tiberius whispered, as they kissed.

Capri wanted so much to believe that, but she knew it was just Tiberius's passion talking. Afraid of trusting him and afraid to trust herself, she pushed away. Tiberius pressed his head against her chest in defeat. Capri kissed the top of his hair, moved off his lap and left.

Tiberius rolled along the highway in his truck. The vintage Wu-Tang CD pounded against the stereo speakers at the highest volume. All Tiberius wanted was to lose himself in the music and forget his rotten day.

He knew everyone at the hospital was aware of the terrible mood he was in. Unfortunately, it couldn't be helped as he'd been walking under a black cloud for the past three days. After talking to Capri, Tiberius was actually at a loss for what to do. He'd never felt so confused about handling a situation with a woman in his life. Of course, over the last several weeks he'd come to realize that Capri wasn't just any woman.

Shaking his head, Tiberius tried to dismiss her from his thoughts. He'd already spent the better part of the week thinking of the two of them in bed. What he needed was a strenuous workout to get rid of some of his pent-up frustration.

Pounding his fist against the steering wheel, he cursed his luck. He'd always considered himself a success with the opposite sex. Finally he had met his match. No sex until marriage, it was simple as that, regardless of whatever doubts she may've been having. Tiberius knew he wanted Capri in his life, but questioned if he was ready for the higher ground of marriage. Of course, it was becoming quite clear that Capri Timmons was a woman he'd do anything for.

The photo spread was a success and the Haize Fragrance group was thrilled. Tiberius and Capri met with everyone involved for a little celebration cocktail party at Rod's office.

Tiberius and Capri were friendly but spent barely five minutes talking to one another. Things had been easy between them following their talk a couple of weeks prior. That strained feeling between them had definitely diminished and they'd changed courses. Still, neither seemed eager to discuss it further.

After half an hour at the get-together, Capri felt she'd faked socializing long enough. She was on her way back to her office when she noticed Rod hailing her from across the room. Not bothering to hide her agitation, she stalked over but had no time to question Rod's sudden need to talk. He drew her into a private conference area where Tiberius sat waiting.

"Capri, Tiberius is working on a project that I think would benefit from a touch of your expertise."

Slowly, Capri eased herself into one of the high-backed chairs at the long table. "How?"

"The project involves a retiring colleague."

"Dr. Thomas?" Capri leaned forward and graced Tiberius with a smile. "How is he?"

He returned the smile, and obviously appreciating her interest. "He's very good."

"So, how can *I* help?"

Tiberius puffed out his cheeks and raised his brows toward Rod.

"I want you to work with him on it. Make it pop. I thought maybe something along the lines of a photographic account of the man's career. Something positive and memorable, not sad and lamenting."

Capri didn't dare say no. Things were weird enough. How could Tiberius just sit there and coolly go along with this? The longer she listened to the two men toss ideas back and forth, however, the more certain she became that this had been Tiberius's *idea* all along.

"How do you want to handle this?" she queried when he asked for her input.

"We still have a few months, so however you want to approach it is fine with me. You're the expert."

Capri's gaze narrowed as she tried to read more into his expression. There was nothing she could draw from it.

"Well, would you want to come here or…"

"Wherever you want to do it, Capri…" He cleared his throat. "It's fine with me."

She stopped fidgeting with the dipping neckline of her pale-blue T-shirt when she saw his stare venture in that direction. "With Rod and Kiva's wedding coming up it might be a bit hectic at first."

"Yeah I know and that's completely understood. I really appreciate your help with this."

"Anytime."

Rod relaxed at the end of the conference table and had the best time watching the syrup flow over the bed of sexual agitation between Capri and Tiberius. He'd put good money on the possibility that his two friends would be lovers before his wedding day.

Chapter 15

Capri had been up since daybreak working on a portfolio for a possible client. Unfortunately, no progress was being made on the project. She'd barely been able to get any sleep the night before, and her thoughts were muddled. The problem? She couldn't keep her mind off Tiberius Evans. The fact that she'd never been totally intimate with a man didn't cause her body to ache any less for him. Capri wanted Tiberius so much in the physical sense, but mainly she had to admit that she was in love with him.

Pushing the unfinished portfolio aside, Capri covered her face with both hands. She sat there motionless for a moment as though she were gathering courage. Finally she stood, tightened the belt around the ice-blue silk robe she wore and left the house.

She pressed her head against Tiberius's front door. At that moment she didn't know if her actions had more to do with love or with lust. The past few months, living next to him, spending time with him, working together on the Haize campaign, had only given heat to the desires she prided herself on resisting. Now her resistance was failing her and she was going to be spending even more time with him until the photo journal for Dr. Thomas was done. She'd gone and fallen in love with Tiberius Evans, and lust was a factor, too. She was so turned around by emotion and only certain of one thing: she wanted him more than she wanted to hold on to anything else.

Capri knocked on the door, but there was no answer. Tiberius's truck was in the yard, so she knew he was home. Gathering the front of her long robe in one hand, she ventured into the backyard. The lights were on in the house, but there was no sign of Tiberius through the glass doors of the kitchen. Taking a chance anyway, Capri tried the handle on the sliding door and it gave.

"Tibe?" she softly called, her throat pounding madly in her chest. "Tiberius?"

There was no answer and Capri hoped he didn't make a habit of leaving his door unlocked all the time. Continuing her journey though the house, she wandered into the spacious sitting room. Of course, there was no sign of Tiberius there either, but Capri did hear what sounded like metal clanging. It came from the far corner of the room.

Heading in that direction, she saw that there was a stairwell leading to a well-lit area. The harsh clanging became louder and, in addition, there was the pounding sound of music. Coming down off the last step, Capri found herself looking out into a state-of-the-art workout room. The fully carpeted gym was filled with all sorts of equipment. Several people could've enjoyed the place at once. However, it was all for one man.

Capri spotted Tiberius at the bench press in the far corner of the room. She hadn't realized that she was holding her breath as she stood rooted to the spot watching him. He must've been lifting well over a hundred and fifty pounds. He performed several repetitions in seemingly effortless motions. When he finally finished and reached for a towel, the muscles in his back rippled and glistened with sweat.

Tiberius wiped the towel across his face, then slid it over his neck and down over his bare chest. The white cotton towel hungrily soaked up the sweat rolling down his body.

As though she were in a daze, Capri walked up behind him and reached out. Tiberius jerked around when he felt the towel being pulled from his hands. The furrow of his brow vanished when he saw Capri. He seemed speechless, and his eyes followed her every move.

Capri completed the task of wiping the sweat away from Tiberius's body. Her dark stare followed the towel's path over the chiseled expanse of his back. Gathering her robe from around her ankles, she stepped in front of Tiberius and knelt before him. She favored his wide chest with the same smooth strokes as his back. Satisfied with the results, she set the towel aside and began pressing soft kisses to the bulging pectorals that contracted beneath her touch. As her soft lips trailed downward across his solid abs, Tiberius leaned his head back and groaned. When Capri's soft caress continued its path downward, Tiberius's eyes snapped open and he grabbed her upper arms.

"Capri, do you know what you're doing?" he asked, his voice raspy with desire.

Capri's gaze was unwavering. "I want you. I want to make love with you."

"I hope you mean that. I'm not in the mood to be teased right now."

"I'm not teasing, I want this," she said softly, sincerely.

"I only want to do this if you're certain," Tiberius warned her. He didn't want her having any doubts.

Capri kept her dark gaze focused on his warm light-brown one. Untying her robe's belt, she pushed the silky material away from her body. "I won't stop you."

Groaning, Tiberius wrapped his hands around Capri's arms and pulled her up before him. She threw her head back and moaned when he took the tip of her breast in his mouth. Capri raced her hands against Tiberius's shoulders and moaned. The expertise of his kiss pulled her into a whirlwind of pleasure.

Tiberius buried his face in the deep valley between her breasts and breathed in. Then, he slid down to glide his mouth across the flat area of her stomach.

Capri threaded her fingers though his hair and gasped when she felt him tonguing her belly button. She pulled his head closer, enjoying the delicious caress.

Meanwhile, Tiberius was thinking he'd never get enough of Capri after having her once. His large hands smoothed over her silken body, circling around to squeeze and caress her full buttocks. He tugged at her hips, bringing her down to straddle his lap. A surprised whimper escaped Capri when she felt the rigid length of his manhood pressing against her. Her small hands kneaded the heavy cords of muscle in his neck while her hips rotated slowly over his huge form.

"Capri…" Tiberius whispered, squeezing her bottom more tightly. His mouth sought hers and he thrust his tongue smoothly inside. The long strokes he applied to the dark cavern of her mouth had them both moaning shamelessly.

Wanting to feel Capri's soft body beneath him, Tiberius stood from the bench, taking her with him. She locked her legs around his waist as he lowered her to the carpet.

Still kissing her madly, Tiberius pulled Capri's arms away from his neck and pressed them above her head. He tore his mouth from hers and slid his lips down the line of her neck. He buried his handsome face in the soft sweet valley under her arm. The unexpected, sensual caress caused her to arch closer to his mouth.

Tiberius's lips moved on and settled once more against her ample cleavage. Very slowly and gently, his tongue swirled around a puckered nipple. His tugs on the firm peak were so pleasurable Capri could feel herself become wetter and more aroused than she had ever been. When Tiberius pulled her arms down to her sides and his lips grazed her womanhood, Capri's eyes widened.

"Shh…relax…" Tiberius whispered as the tip of his tongue slowly entered her.

Capri's eyes fluttered shut as she let the mastery of Tiberius's intimate caresses take over. His tongue delved deeply inside her and every part of her body quivered.

Tiberius let go of Capri's arms to take her hips in a firm hold. His tongue caressed her more thoroughly and her soft cries became louder. He alternated between thrusting his tongue smoothly inside her and nipping at the satiny petals of her womanhood with his perfect teeth. He kissed the insides of her thighs, smiling when he saw the muscles contracting there.

He cupped Capri's buttocks and pulled her toward him. The action gave his lips and tongue more room to explore. Capri thought she'd go mad from the indescribable pleasure.

When Tiberius pulled his mouth away, Capri moaned her disappointment. Ignoring her, he trailed wet kisses up the length of her body before his mouth settled over hers once more.

Capri was so entranced by the taste of herself on Tiberius's lips that she didn't notice his fingers traveling toward the juncture of her thighs. The tip of his index finger trailed her there, before he let his middle finger push ahead.

Capri tensed the moment she felt him there. Tiberius didn't veer from his task, throwing a heavy leg across her thigh to prevent her from closing on him. His finger rotated inside her until he felt her relax just slightly. He deepened the caress and she moaned in response. Tiberius's fingers were as persuasive as his mouth, and Capri was in heaven.

Tiberius could feel her becoming wetter with each rotation of his fingers. He didn't want to rush things, but it was becoming increasingly difficult for him to hold back. Of course, he knew this couldn't happen without protection. Though he hated to ruin the moment, he knew precautions needed to be taken. Groaning, he held her close and lifted her from the floor. Capri's lashes fluttered open in surprise.

"Shh…everything's okay. We're just going upstairs," he assured her.

Soon they were entering his bedroom and Tiberius lowered Capri to his bed. The masculine surroundings caused Capri to tense a little, but Tiberius's touch immediately relaxed her.

When Capri's fingers grazed the rigid bulge between his legs,

Tiberius knew he couldn't wait any longer. Capri had already begun pulling down the shorts he wore. She was eager to feel him without the barrier of clothes.

Tiberius helped her pull his shorts away. Capri opened her eyes when she felt him. His throbbing length felt like a long, steel bar sheathed in silk. She caressed him, trying to memorize every inch. Tiberius's long lashes closed as he enjoyed the innocent caress. Before Capri could unknowingly bring an end to the moment, he pulled away. He reached for the condoms in his nightstand and adjusted the protection. Then, as he stared into Capri's lovely face, he positioned the tip of his long shaft against her.

"Look at me," he whispered, watching her doe eyes raise to his face. "I don't want to hurt you, so I'll be as gentle as possible."

Capri nodded as she lifted her head for another kiss. Tiberius complied, praying she wouldn't bite him when he took her.

His movement was slow and loving. After a few moments, he began to move a bit faster and Capri's body slowly became pliant beneath him. Tiberius groaned and buried his face in the crook of her neck. The pleasure was unbelievable and the more relaxed Capri became, the deeper Tiberius made his strokes.

She started moving her hips in tiny circular motions. She was uncertain, but when Tiberius moaned in response to each movement, her confidence grew. Soon, they had found a mutual rhythm and the pleasure that arose was incredible.

Tiberius was amazed at how gentle he could be with Capri when he was so hungry for her. He introduced her to various positions, each more sensual than the last. Capri realized with a great deal of delight that she was an eager student. She was content to learn as much as she could from Tiberius for the rest of the day.

The next morning, Tiberius forced his eyes open. He was completely drained from the night before. He felt good though, very good considering how late it was when he and Capri went to sleep.

Turning on his side, Tiberius propped one hand along the side of his face and stared down at her where she lay next to him. His sexy, light stare slid over her nude honey-toned body. *God, last night with her was incredible,* he thought. All his daydreams about them together were nothing compared to the real thing.

In all honesty, he'd thought having her would finally purge his desire. It had done just the opposite. He wanted her more than ever.

Damn, what's wrong with me? Tiberius wondered, shaking his head as if to clear it.

Just then, Capri turned in her sleep. As she snuggled deeper into the covers, her eyes opened and she looked up at Tiberius. She took a long stretch, wiggling her fingers at him in a lazy greeting.

"How do you feel?" Tiberius questioned, his sleek dark brow drawn in concern.

Capri smiled. "Good…very good."

"I hope I didn't hurt you."

Capri understood what he meant, but didn't comment. Instead, she slid her arms around his neck and pulled him close. Tiberius's long lashes closed over the wells of his eyes, as Capri pressed soft kisses to the strong column of his neck. He wasn't about to resist her sensuous offer.

Capri and Tiberius frequently made plans to be together. Though their careers at times made that difficult, they were determined. More than anything, they enjoyed spending time together and learning more about each other. Even in the midst of organizing the photo layout for Dr. Thomas it was clear they were enjoying the chore far more than they should have.

Each day, Capri could feel herself becoming more attracted to Tiberius. Tiberius had yet to say anything along those lines. He had told her that she was the only one he wanted to see, but for the time being, she would have to be content with that. Capri wasn't naive, though. Of course Tiberius's company was something she'd grown to treasure, but she couldn't become too attached. It would only make things harder when he finally told her it wouldn't last.

"Dammit," Capri hissed, realizing she'd gotten lost in her thoughts while sitting in her truck. Glancing at her watch, she prayed Tiberius hadn't been waiting too long inside the restaurant. Capri hopped out of the Pathfinder and turned to lock the door. As she did so, an arm slid neatly around her waist.

"Sorry I'm late."

Capri smiled at the deep, mellow voice, behind her. "I was just going to tell you the same thing," she admitted, turning to face Tiberius.

He tilted his head to one side and glared at her. "What's wrong?"

Capri's wide, dark gaze lowered. "Nothing."

"You sure?"

Capri sighed and took his arm. "I'm positive. Come on."

"So when can we get together for dinner?"

Capri tried to swallow past her laughter. "We aren't even through with lunch yet."

Tiberius propped one finger against his temple. "I like to plan ahead."

"Mmm-hmm…" Capri smiled. "Well, I don't know when I'll get out of the studio, but I'll call you."

Lunch and conversation were wonderful. As usual, Capri and Tiberius found plenty to discuss. In fact, they were so engrossed with one another they weren't aware that Clarissa Harris was seated just a few tables away, her brown eyes filled with unmistakable vengeance.

"Where is he?" Capri sighed and put the phone down. It was just after 8:00 p.m. and she'd just arrived home. There was no answer at Tiberius's house, but she saw his truck in the driveway.

Setting her camera case and portfolio on the coffee table, Capri decided to head next door. Once she'd gotten to the front door and rung the bell, she slipped out of her brown wide-strapped mules. She wiggled her toes on the large welcome mat and yawned. After a long, exhausting day, all she wanted to do was eat and go to sleep. Still, there was something she wanted to discuss with Tiberius, and though every part of her brain shrieked that it was a bad idea she knew she had to put it on the table.

Of course, Tiberius had other plans. As soon as he opened the front door, he grabbed Capri's waist and pulled her inside. His massive hands cupped her hips and he held her close. Capri moaned in response when she felt the rigid proof of his arousal pressing against her.

Tiberius dipped his head and thrust his tongue between her parted lips. The kiss was long, deep and slow. Tiberius moaned, as his fingers went to Capri's silk shirt and he began to unbutton it.

Capri would've loved to continue the sensual scene, but what she had to say was best said up front. "Tibe, wait a minute," she whispered beneath the passionate kiss.

"What for?" he grumbled, his mind on getting Capri out of her clothes.

Capri brought her hands up to the front of her blouse and started to rebutton it. "Can we talk first?"

"Later."

"Tibe—"

"Shh…I want this first," he told her, his fingers going to the zipper of her white bellbottoms.

"We can do *this* later…" Capri coolly replied, though her voice rose a little.

"What's wrong?"

"I need to talk."

"About?"

Capri averted her gaze. "It's gonna upset you."

Tiberius sighed and pushed one hand through his hair. "Impossible. I can't possibly be any more upset than I already am."

"All right. It's about us…"

"Really?"

She rolled her eyes in response to the sarcasm rolling from his voice. "This isn't easy, Tibe."

"It'll be a lot easier once you say it."

"Somehow I doubt that," she murmured.

"Capri!"

"Okay! I just don't want you to think I expect anything from you."

The wicked scowl on Tiberius's handsome face deepened. He let her move by him and watched her, disbelief slowly filling his eyes.

"We've made love several times, and I, um, you know what my opinions were about sex. A lot of that has changed, but a lot of it hasn't. Still, I don't want to you think I expect you to…" She let her voice trail away until she regained her momentum. "It's just that I know the novelty of this will wear off eventually and I'll just become another girl you slept with."

Without a word, Tiberius rolled his eyes away from her and headed out of the foyer.

Capri propped her hands on her hips and glared at his retreating figure. "Where are you going?"

"To fix dinner!"

Capri closed her eyes and counted to ten. Then she followed him. "We need to talk about this, don't you think?"

Tiberius stormed into the kitchen and pulled the refrigerator door open. "I actually don't."

Capri leaned against the kitchen island and watched him slam bowls on the counter. "I know this seems like it's coming out of nowhere—"

"Hmph."

She sighed. "Look, I've had a rough day, Tiberius, and this has been on my mind for most of it. You would've figured that out soon enough, so I thought I should at least be up-front enough to tell you."

"Thanks."

"Tibe, please don't do this. Nothing's gonna come from you being angry."

"I'm willing to go with it for a while." The pointed look Tiberius sent her way clearly stated that now was not the time to go into further discussion.

Capri was beginning to agree. "Can't you see where I'm coming from? Just a little?"

Tiberius slammed his fist to the table, causing the glasses there to rattle. "Do you really think that you're the only one with morals? Did you ever stop to think it could've been about more than that for me?"

Capri had no comeback. She didn't need one when the answer to his question was all over her face.

Tiberius ran both hands over his face. "Do you know how many virgins I've slept with?"

Capri looked away. "I prefer not to."

"You're the first and the only, I hope. So I'm just as clueless about what to do here as you are."

Capri's mouth formed an O of surprise. "Tibe—"

Tiberius waved his hand as if to dismiss her. "You need to go, Capri."

When he heard the front door close, he knew he should've gone after her. Unfortunately, he had no idea what to say once he caught her.

Chapter 16

"So you're just gonna close the door on what could be a great relationship? Because of what you *think* he's thinking?"

Capri rolled her eyes and buried her head beneath the pillow on Pepper's bed. She was so heated after the fight with Tiberius that she'd driven into the city and headed to her best friend's apartment. "It was so stupid even to go to him with it and to top it all off I was completely wrong."

"How'd you guys leave things?"

"Not well."

Pepper trudged across her bedroom and pulled the pillows away from Capri. "So what now?"

Capri ran her hands through her tousled curls and glared at Pepper. "I don't know. I guess I didn't think he'd get so upset by it."

Pepper sat on the bed and propped her elbows on her knees. "So his feelings are stronger than you thought they could be, and I'm thinking yours are, too."

"I suppose."

"Have you told him how you feel. How you really feel?"

"I don't know if he'll even believe me now."

"Cap—"

"Look, Pepper, I still don't want to pressure Tiberius into admitting anything. I knew where things stood with him from the jump, and at least he's been up front about it. Meanwhile, I still can't admit that I was having my *issues* well before anything serious began between us."

"So what's the truth, then?"

Capri pressed the heels of her hands against her eyes. "I guess I've been psyching myself up to be hurt by him." She shook her head. "So I won't be so devastated when…if it happens. So…staying true to form, I'm once again lying to myself."

Pepper toyed with the frilly edge of her peach comforter. "But do you believe *him?*"

"I want to but…"

"But you're afraid," Pepper guessed and tousled her friend's curls. "You know, he just might surprise you."

Capri shrugged and buried her face back into the pillows for comfort.

It took Capri three days to decide to make the first move and contact Tiberius. She at least owed it to herself to find out if there was any reason for her to continue the relationship—any reason to give more of herself than she already had. Unfortunately, she was terribly afraid of saying the wrong thing again, especially when her feelings for Tiberius were becoming so strong.

Luckily, she was able to put all of that behind her the next morning when she went next door to Tiberius's house. Sighing nervously, Capri smoothed her hands over her low-riding denim shorts and rang the doorbell. Upon a closer look, she noticed that the front door was slightly ajar. Frowning, she pushed it open and stuck her head inside.

"Tibe?" she called, waiting for some response. When there was none, she assumed he'd left the door open again. Instead of doing any further investigating, she decided to leave. She was about to close the door when something on the floor caught her eye.

Very slowly, she walked into the foyer and knelt to pick up the piece of material. With a sharp gasp she realized it was a half slip.

Capri pressed her lips together and looked toward the carpeted stairway. It was draped with women's clothing. As if in a daze, she collected the pieces and made her way to the top of the stairway. The trail led right to Tiberius's room. Judging from the ton of women's garb she'd collected, it didn't take a genius to figure Tiberius had found someone else to soothe his urges.

Tiberius stretched his nude body between the sheets. His eyes snapped open and he immediately sensed he wasn't alone in the room. Squinting slightly, he tried to make out the figure at the foot of the bed. "Capri?" he murmured, pushing himself up.

Capri felt her chest ache as she struggled to contain her tears. Storming over to the bed, she threw the clothes in his face. "Looks like you got your cheap, corny lines to work on somebody else, too," she said and left the room.

"Capri!" Tiberius called, not about to let her get away. He jumped out of bed and went after her. She was rushing down the stairway, but he grabbed her before she got too far. "What is this?"

Tears blurred Capri's vision and she shook her head. "I came over here to talk to you about that stupid argument. I've been so turned around and I should've stayed and hashed it out with you the other day instead of letting it turn into... I guess it doesn't matter now."

"Would you please tell me what's going on?" Tiberius slowly requested, his heart racing. Capri's soft weeping was tearing him apart.

"It doesn't matter, Tibe. It doesn't matter at all," she told him, trying to save face. Too upset to say anything more, she pulled away from him and ran out of the house.

Tiberius filled the air with a string of curses. Stomping back to his room, he went over to the bed and picked up one of the flimsy pieces of lingerie. A murderous look fell over his face as he stared at the garment.

"Clarissa."

Chapter 17

"Capri, honey, do you ever stop working?"

Capri pulled her head out of the stack of reports on her desk and looked up. Kiva was leaning against the doorjamb, a wide grin on her lips. "Hmm, I wonder why that is?"

Capri shrugged. "Well, moving for one, and then I tripped on that broken step, and let's not forget that mess with Avery Erikson."

"Right. I think you left something out, though."

"I don't think so," Capri said, frowning slightly.

"What about Tiberius?"

Capri rolled her eyes and remained silent.

"What's that look about?"

"Nothing."

"Capri…"

"Kiva, please, I really can't talk about it."

Kiva knew not to push, so she turned her attention to the white envelope she held. "Well, I actually came to give you this."

Capri took the envelope and frowned. "What's this?"

"Open it."

Doing as she was told, Capri examined the contents. Her frown turned into a smile when she realized it was the wedding invitation. "I was wondering when I'd get this."

"I hope you'll be there, even though Tiberius is on the guest list, too."

"Don't even pull that," Capri warned, standing and walking from behind the desk. "You know I'll be there." She pulled Kiva close for a hug. Capri read over the invitation again, and this time her brow rose slightly. "A wedding on a yacht?" she questioned.

Kiva's eyes widened. "Honey, yes! A friend of Rod's is letting us use it for the occasion."

"Going all out, aren't we?"

"Of course," Kiva raved. "I've waited a long time for Rod and I'm determined to do this right."

"I hear that."

Kiva decided to ignore the pensive look on Capri's face. "Before I forget, I need to tell you to bring a change of clothes."

"Change of clothes?"

"Mmm-hmm. We're gonna dock in the Keys so Rod and I can get off for our honeymoon in Jamaica."

Capri shook her head, pulling Kiva close again. "I must say I'm impressed."

"I was hoping you would be." Kiva laughed.

Capri squeezed her eyes shut tight and tried to ward off her own special memories of time spent in the alluring Keys.

"Clarissa Harris Designs."

Tiberius practically snarled when he heard Clarissa's perky voice on the phone. "How the hell did you get inside my house?"

"Tiberius?"

"What the hell were you doing in my house, Clarissa?"

In spite of the fierce tone of Tiberius's voice, Clarissa laughed. "I think you know what I was doing in there."

"How'd you get in?"

Clarissa shrugged. "I must've forgotten to return your key when I left."

"You conniving—" Tiberius stopped himself from uttering the rest of the phrase.

Clarissa blinked and didn't need him to finish, as she'd already guessed what was next. She sat up a little straighter behind her desk.

Tiberius had never used such language, even when they'd had their most terrible arguments. "Come on, Tiberius, what's the big deal?"

"The woman I love found that mess in my house. I probably lost her over your stupidity."

"The woman you love? I must be hearing you wrong."

"You're not."

"Who is she? The cute little busty one I saw you with the other day at Gravy's Seafood?"

"Look, Clarissa, just return my key and keep your ass out of my house."

"Tibe, I—"

"Just do what I tell you. I mean it, Clarissa. Don't push me on this," Tiberius growled.

When the phone slapped down in Clarissa's ear, her entire body jerked in reaction to it. If she didn't know better, she could've sworn she was talking to a different man.

For the fifth time since she'd sat down at the table, Capri's eyes slid across the dining room. She'd been waiting for Pepper who was having lunch with her. Unfortunately, Capri had arrived early and discovered that Tiberius was there as well. Each time she looked up he was watching her.

Though she hated how edgy he was making her feel, she knew she couldn't leave. All she could think of was that morning in his house. The memories kept her glued to her chair.

Capri was angrier with herself than anyone else. She hated the fact that she'd shared some of the most private things about life with Tiberius. She'd completely lowered her defenses and lost control. Still, she had no regrets. He was what she'd wanted then. Who was she kidding? He was what she wanted *now*.

Clearing her throat, Capri reached for her glass of tea. She drank the entire glass and munched on the small square cubes of ice at the bottom.

Tiberius, who had been having lunch with a few colleagues, was wrapping up his meeting. When he shook hands and waved off the other three doctors, he tossed back the rest of his drink. Then he headed across the dining room.

"We're gonna be grandparents."

Capri set her glass down and looked up at Tiberius. Her lovely face was a picture of confusion. "Excuse me?"

Tiberius pushed one hand into the pocket of his maroon trousers and smiled. "Droopey's expecting."

"Expecting what?" Capri asked, still dumbfounded. That, plus the fact that she couldn't believe she was talking to him after so many days.

"Droopey's pregnant."

Capri's dark eyes lit up at the news. "Lewey and Droopey made babies."

Tiberius's hazel gaze grew more intense as he watched her. Pulling his hand from his pocket, he took a seat at the table and noticed the bright smile on Capri's face leave, to be replaced by a look of uncertainty. "What's wrong?" he asked.

Capri swallowed and held her hands out. "I'm sorry about this. I should've kept him better restrained."

Tiberius frowned a little and shrugged his shoulder. "Ah, don't worry about it," he said, with a careless wave. "Restrained or not, he wouldn't have been able to resist my girl."

Capri laughed. "No, I think you've got that backwards. See, it's Droopey who couldn't resist my big guy."

Tiberius's deep laughter rumbled to the surface and, for a moment, they teased each other about whose dog was more irresistible. Unfortunately, the laughter soon ceased and silence settled between them.

"Capri, about what you saw—"

"Tibe, please, you don't have to."

"I want to. I need to talk to you about this."

Capri took a deep breath and lowered her eyes to study the table. "Tibe, I really can't talk about this with you now."

"When then?" he asked, upset by her unwillingness to hear him out.

Capri twirled a lock of hair around her finger. "I don't know, Tibe, but I can't talk about it now because I'm meeting Pepper for lunch."

Tiberius turned around and followed the line of Capri's gaze. He saw Pepper heading toward the table and gave a disappointed smile. "We can't keep ignoring each other, Capri."

Capri looked right into his light eyes but couldn't respond.

"Hello, Tiberius," Pepper said as she stood next to the table.

Tiberius got out of the chair and held it for Pepper.

"Good to see you, Pepper." He gave her a dazzling dimpled smile. Turning back to Capri he nodded. "I'll be seeing you."

"I know I just interrupted something. What was it?" Pepper asked, as soon as Tiberius walked away.

Capri pressed her palm to her forehead and sighed. "I guess he took our argument more seriously than I thought. He slept with another woman."

Pepper's mouth dropped open. "What?"

"Her clothes were draped over his stairway."

"Oh," Pepper softly replied. "Well, you never know. He still might have a good explanation—though I have no idea what it could be. Still, maybe you should hear him out."

"I don't know."

"I assume he was trying to explain before I got here?"

"You assume correctly."

Pepper frowned. "Well?"

"Well, what?"

"You're not giving me anything here."

"Pepper I just don't think I have the nerve to talk to him. I was standing in his bedroom with some other woman's lingerie lying all around and even then I didn't believe what I was seeing, that he would do that. Stupid, huh?" Capri felt her lashes flutter at the memory.

Pepper leaned back in her chair and regarded her best friend with a thoughtful stare. For the first time in a long time, she had no clue what to say.

Chapter 18

"Wow! What's all this?" Capri wondered using her hand to brim her eyes against the sun when she jumped from the Navigator.

Tiberius took in all of the hubbub when he left the driver's side. "No idea. Felicity didn't mention anything when I called about coming out."

Capri stood in awe of all the people mulling about the property. She and Tiberius had returned to Alan and Felicity Thomas's Key Biscayne estate against their better judgment, but they had a job to do. Grimacing, Capri turned to fix Tiberius with a soft look.

"Look, thanks for coming out here. I know you hadn't planned on this, but I really think we'll benefit from a second visit."

"I still don't see the point of looking for more photos when the hospital's got plenty already."

Capri was already nodding at his point. "I'm looking for intimacy."

Tiberius blinked. "Did you say intimacy?"

"I did."

"You're gonna have to explain that one."

Capri stood on the Navigator's step rail in order to face him more directly. "What I'm looking for are photos that say something about his life, his family, his hobbies, his passions…the things that make it all worthwhile." She spread her hands across the roof of the SUV. "The hospital shots speak to his passion, of course, but the photos I want now will speak to his soul."

"Learn somethin' new every day, I guess." Tiberius grinned and smoothed the back of his hand across his jaw. "I truly had no idea that so much thought went into choosing a picture."

"What can I say? It's a science."

"And you're an extremely talented scientist."

"I do what I can." Capri shrugged, and slanted him a saucy wink before she jumped off the step rail.

Tiberius maintained his stance near the Navigator. His gaze was focused and probing as he studied her, admiring her skill as much as he admired the sparkle in her dark eyes when she spoke about her work.

"Tiberius? Capri? Oh I'm just tickled y'all could make it out!"

Felicity Thomas hurried down the white brick steps leading onto the horseshoe drive. She clapped and giggled so enthusiastically that Tiberius and Capri exchanged glances and silently decided she was just a bit too thrilled by their arrival.

"I'm afraid I wasn't very up-front with you earlier, Tiberius."

"Is that right?" Tiberius leaned down to kiss the woman's cheek.

Felicity's vibrant blue stare narrowed playfully. "I did have an ulterior motive for wanting you two back out here again."

"Such as?" Capri asked when it was her turn to kiss Felicity's cheek.

"I don't think I told you that Al and I are celebrating our golden anniversary this weekend."

Capri scanned the sea of bodies roaming the grounds. "And all these people are preparing for the party?"

"Bingo!"

"Felicity—"

"Now I won't take 'no' for an answer. You two are here and here you'll remain until the last bottle of champagne is drained."

For a sixty-eight-year-old woman, Felicity Thomas was formidable when the issue of partying was at stake.

"Well, we've got nothing to wear," Capri tried, glancing down at her hip-hugging beige short suit and then over at Tiberius's sagging jeans and throwback Dolphins jersey. "We can't go like this."

"No worries, darlin'. Why, there are plenty of sweet li'l shops right here in Biscayne, isn't that right, Tiberius?"

Felicity's enthusiasm was apparently contagious, for Tiberius was grinning almost as broadly as she was. "That's right."

"But—"

"Now now, Capri. *Technically* you're here on business and that's what expense reports are for, right?"

"Right." Capri's response was low. While she rarely passed on a chance to shop, she didn't know how eager she was for an impromptu trip right on the heels of the Keys. It all may turn out to be a bit more than she needed.

Tiberius, however, was quite sold on the idea of staying simply because he craved the time alone with Capri. "This could be just what you need."

Capri spared a quick look at Felicity before glaring at Tiberius. "What *I* need?"

"Photos with intimacy?" he reminded her, and moved around to the front of his truck. "Weekend like this'll give you a lot of photo ops, won't it?"

Capri closed her eyes, unable to argue his point. "Good thing I never leave home without it," she said as she grabbed her camera bag from the backseat.

There were indeed several photo ops, and Capri began shooting the moment they headed toward the house.

"Felicity, I don't know how you do this, organizing parties almost right on top of one another."

"Oh, honey, I enjoy it so. Always have."

Capri captured a shot of an elaborate ice sculpture. "I'd go crazy trying to organize all this."

"Life of a doctor's wife, sweetie." Felicity gave a surprisingly youthful twist of her hips. "You'll find that out soon enough."

Capri was struck silent then and ceased working with the lens of her wide angle. She risked a glance a Tiberius and celebrated the fact that he hadn't heard the remark.

The threesome headed inside the house with Capri snapping shots the whole time. She'd taken almost a full roll by the time they were ascending the magnificent spiral stairway. Felicity chatted nonstop and even mentioned the weather, noting a tropical storm in the forecast that might set down upon them.

"Might make your party a little difficult," Tiberius warned.

"Oh no. If anything I'm looking forward to it even more. There's somethin' cozy about partying in the midst of a torrential downpour."

Capri shook her head, though she adored the older woman's strong romantic streak.

"Yes, I *do* enjoy overnight affairs." Felicity sighed, still surprisingly energetic once they'd cleared the staircase. "The idea of having my guests under the same roof makes the evening more magical. Now let's see…"

Tiberius and Capri followed along like obedient children as Felicity seemed to decide on and change her mind against entering at least three doors. Clearly having certain guests in the same *room* made the lady of the house feel wonderful as well, for she settled Capri and Tiberius in a breathtaking suite. The lavish digs came complete with a stunning view of the Atlantic.

"Now the party will get underway around seven-thirty or eight. Tiberius knows where all the shops are." Her eyes were full of devilment as she watched them. "You two have fun. I'll see you later."

"Not very subtle, is she?" Capri spoke some forty seconds after the door closed behind Felicity.

Tiberius massaged his neck. "She never has been. Capri, I'm sorry about this. I can easily snag another room—"

"No don't." Capri shrugged the camera bag strap from her shoulder. "I don't mind. Really."

Tiberius winced. "Yeah, but that sofa across the room isn't gonna suit me and there's no way I'm gonna let you sleep on it."

"We *can* share the bed, you know?"

Tiberius felt his jaw drop to the floor. "Share it?" He massaged his forehead as she nodded.

"Oh, Tibe, please. We're adults. I think we can share a bed."

"You're serious, aren't you?" Tiberius watched in disbelief as she coolly set out to inspect the room. "Do you know what's bound to happen between us in here? What sure as hell *will* happen if we're in the same bed?"

"It's happened before…" Capri let out a whistle at the walk-in closet. "Several times."

Tiberius groaned. Closing his eyes, he was desperate to put distance between them.

Realizing that the conversation had no hope of reaching a satisfactory conclusion, Capri set out to inspect her camera bag. When she looked up after a few moments, Tiberius's gaze was focused right on her. She thanked the clap of thunder that tugged his attention away from her momentarily.

He jingled keys in his pocket. "We better bounce if we plan to shop before this storm hits."

Several guests had arrived in the time it took for Capri and Tiberius to shop for their outfits and other necessities for the overnight stay. When they returned to the Thomas's estate, Tiberius was immediately pulled aside by his colleagues and Capri socialized for a moment before deciding to make her escape to the bedroom where she planned to take advantage of the privacy and try on her gown again.

The dress fitted like a dream and Capri celebrated her luck—a new frock out of the blue, and charged to Grant and Sheilds, no less. Life was good.

Still, her ease faded a bit as she looked around the gorgeous room. Tiberius was right, she thought. There was no way they could be in the same room and not behave like two…well, adults. Capri cleared her throat and felt her legs grow weak at the mere thought of it. She'd certainly offer no protest were it to happen. There was still so much between them though, and the blame for it lay right at her feet. Before *any adult* activities occurred between them, there were other things that needed to be settled.

Capri was still admiring her dress when Tiberius walked into the room. It would have been the perfect time to delve right into the conversation they needed to have, but the opportunity didn't have the chance to present itself. The door slammed behind Tiberius and seconds later Capri was in his arms.

His mouth came down upon hers hard in a thoroughly anguished kiss. Capri met the force of Tiberius with wild enthusiasm and curved her hands around his face and neck. Tiberius's hands were everywhere, anywhere they could graze her bare skin. The cut of the dress provided plenty of that and then some. A row of tiny coral-colored buttons began at her hip and snaked up her side to disappear beneath her bare arm. Her other arm was covered by a long sleeve, the cuff shielding her wrist and half of her hand from view. The lace bodice molded to her ample bustline, baring a good portion to Tiberius's gaze. His thumbs worked across her nipples causing them to strain fiercely against the binding material.

Reluctantly, Capri drew a hand from his soft hair to cover his where he'd begun to tug at the tiny buttons along the side of the dress. Breathing heavily, he pressed his mouth back on to hers and fought to calm himself.

"We should head back downstairs before things get too heated. Felicity… She, um…brought some albums down for us to look through. I'll be in the den off the foyer when you come down." He brushed a fast kiss across Capri's mouth and left the room as coolly as he'd entered.

The lower level had settled down considerably when Capri descended the stairs fifteen minutes later. Everyone had apparently journeyed to their respective rooms in order to escape the approaching storm and the dark clouds and wind it had already produced. Everyone, that is, except for Tiberius and Capri.

She found him on a sofa in the den, frowning down into a page of a mammoth-sized album.

"Knock, knock."

Tiberius grinned but didn't look up. "Dig in." He waved a hand toward the other four albums and loose photos on the oak coffee table. "There's plenty."

Capri was ready to see what they had and eagerly joined Tiberius on the sofa. They worked in comfortable silence for a long while. Rain and a bit of lightning were soon coming down quite steadily but they simply made the atmosphere more soothing. Capri celebrated the fact that her hunch was correct, as the photos contained in the albums held the exact *intimacy* she was looking for. During her critical survey of the photos, however, Capri found herself surveying another image. This was a mental image, one she discovered she hadn't observed with enough detail the first time around. More time passed and Capri found herself breaking the silence that surrounded them.

"I'm sorry, Tibe."

He seemed to freeze at the sound of her words. More than a little confused, he remained focused on the photo in his hand, but he didn't really see it.

Capri tossed the picture she held onto the coffee table. "I shouldn't have made you think you owed me any explanations about your intentions or about my insecurities. Not when it was so obvious that Clarissa set the whole thing up."

"Obvious?"

She graced him with her dimpled smile. "Tibe, I'm a photographer. I've staged enough phony love scenes for shoots to know the difference between what's real and what's not and still this got right past me." Flopping back on the sofa, Capri shook her head. "She set it up. I couldn't see it then but I think inside I knew almost from the minute I walked up the stairs."

"I love you."

Capri laughed, not hearing Tiberius. "I shouldn't have taken so long to see it."

Tiberius rolled his eyes and tapped a photo against his palm. "I love you."

Sobering then, Capri studied him closely and understood that his declaration of love had nothing to do with her discovery of Clarissa Harris's motives. "Tibe, you don't have to—"

"I love you and I'm scared."

This last statement threw her and the shock was etched in every angle of her expression.

Tossing aside his photo, Tiberius grinned at her reaction. "Now you can understand how I felt when you told me you were a virgin."

Capri had never heard a man admit to being scared and didn't think it was even possible. Moreover, she certainly hadn't thought it was possible that she'd ever hear Tiberius Evans say it. She prayed he'd at least do her the honor of telling her why. Thankfully he didn't make her wait long.

"My parents divorced four years ago," Tiberius said as he reached for a stack of photos and began to shuffle through them in an absent manner. "Know why they stayed together?" He spared her a weary glance. "My grandparents wanted me to have a real family. With two happy parents and a happy little home."

He chuckled, but Capri could hear more pain fueling the gesture than humor.

"They threatened to cut my parents out of the will if they split up. They only had to stay together until I graduated high school but they toughed it out until my grandmother passed." He tossed the photos to the table. "Guess they didn't want to risk her changing her mind."

"Tibe," Capri whispered.

"I didn't even know all this until my grandmother's funeral." He massaged the bridge of his nose. "They were fighting like cats and dogs, the usual. I cursed them out right there in my grandmother's bedroom and asked why they even bothered. They sure as hell told me why.

"I was a one-night stand and neither side wanted the black mark of a child born out of wedlock doing damage to their family names." A smirk triggered his dimple. "At least that's the way my mom's parents saw it. My dad's folks, my grandparents," he clarified as if to make a point of recognizing Tiberius and Janice Evans as his only grandparents, "they loved me. You don't know how many nights I sat in my room and wished *they* could've been my parents."

He shrugged. "You know the funny part? I've seen worse relationships. Way worse. I guess that's part of the reason I became an obstetrician—something about seeing those couples about to become parents and feeling so damn happy about it. Parents crazy with excitement. I never even had the nerve to ask my folks if they were ever just a little happy when they were pregnant with me."

Capri squeezed his hand. "I'm sure they were. I'm sure they were," she repeated when he squeezed back and tugged her close to him. They held on to each other for the longest time.

"Oh, sorry," Capri whispered the hushed apology and edged closer to the counter when Tiberius walked into the bathroom and patted her waist in a silent request that she make room.

"You're fine. I only wanted to brush my teeth." He shook the slender black leather valise he'd brought in with him.

They were preparing for the party, set to begin shortly. Capri continued to pin her curls while Tiberius brushed. They worked at their individual tasks for several minutes but Capri was first to let her gaze stray. The muscles that flexed and rippled in his arms and back caught and held her stare.

"Capri?"

She wasn't even making a pretense at working on her hair then. She stared as if mesmerized by the honey tone of his skin, his back made out of muscle, his lean waist, and below...

"Capri?" Tiberius spoke through a mouth full of toothpaste. "You okay?"

She caught herself before he had to ask again. "Sorry."

He rinsed his mouth and looked at her again. "You all right?"

"Yeah, yeah, I'm fine." She finished with her hair and leaned her hip against the counter. "Are *you* all right?"

He didn't pretend to misunderstand her question and nodded. "I'm good. Didn't mean to lay all that on you yesterday. Guess I should apologize, too."

"No." Capri allowed her eyes to stray once more as he reached for a hand towel off the top shelf of the linen rack. "No you sounded like you needed to get that off of your...chest."

Tiberius was so preoccupied by thoughts of the conversation that he didn't notice the pure hunger in Capri's eyes as she scanned his bare torso.

"I never told anyone that."

She snapped to and graced him with a soft smile. "I'm glad I was there."

Tiberius leaned against the other end of the counter and returned her smile. "Please don't tell Rod I got so heavy, okay?"

"My lips are sealed."

His expression was serious when he stepped close. "Thank you." He kissed her forehead and left the bathroom.

Chapter 19

Tropical Storm Bettina raged into the night but didn't have a negative effect on the party. If anything, the dreariness of the day seemed to accentuate the allure of the festivities. Golden light beamed from almost every area of the lovely home.

Capri was entranced, feeling as though she was in the middle of paradise. She and Tiberius were dancing again in their special spot with that glorious view of the Atlantic. She inhaled the fabulously sexy scent of his cologne and wondered if he realized he hadn't let go of her since they headed down into the party.

Not that she was complaining. There was something possessive yet protective in his touch. Capri thought back to the previous day. They'd been so on edge about the sleeping arrangements. When they returned to the suite, however, not only did they fall asleep but they were fully clothed. Smiling, Capri snuggled deeper into the dance as she remembered.

"Sleepy?" Tiberius inquired, chuckling when she looked up and fixed him with a knowing glare. Clearly she was recalling the last time they were there in similar circumstances.

"Not yet," Capri intimated the same response she'd once given.

"Bored?"

"Not *even*."

Mutual laughter flooded between them. When they looked up at each other again though, all traces of humor were gone. In place of it was the need that seemed to always rest between them. Unmindful then of where they were or who may be watching, their lips met in a crushing kiss.

Tiberius's tongue thrust hungrily past her lips. "Capri…"

"I know…"

They left the party behind and returned to the room, again kissing madly before the doors even closed behind them. Capri didn't pause to mourn the destruction of her dress as buttons popped and material snagged beneath Tiberius's strong fingers. When she was nude in his arms, he kept her against the wall nearest the door.

His mouth blazed a heated wet trail across her chest. He stopped to torture her firming nipples with several moments of ravenous suckling before traveling onward. His hands molded to her bottom to keep her in place when he tongued her bellybutton and nuzzled his nose across the satiny bare skin above her womanhood.

Capri could have wilted from pleasure when he nibbled her extra-sensitive bud of flesh before soothing it with his tongue. His grip upon her buttocks firmed as he held her higher to accommodate the journey of his tongue. She sobbed his name as he made love to her with his mouth. She wanted to share the waves of satisfaction with him but he gave her no chance.

Capri played the passive role for only a short while longer. Then she drew strength from her desire, determined to see him out of the gorgeous tux he was wearing. Once he was as nude as she, they kissed their way to the bed, laughing as they fell upon it.

"Capri…" Tiberius raked his fingers through her hair as she began to lavish him with a similar oral treat to the one he'd just given her.

The harsh thundering of the storm had resumed and seemed to add more intensity to the scene. Capri felt starved for Tiberius and adored the way he responded to her touch. When he suddenly pulled her up and over his body she was confused. For Tiberius, his restraint was reaching its end and he needed to be inside her.

Capri tugged at her lip as he drew a condom packet from beneath one of the many pillows lining the headboard. She took the package and handled the task of putting the protection in place. Flashes of lightning filled the room as they made love to each other. Capri covered his hands with hers as they were cupped over her breasts while she rode his body. She took everything he had to give and he of course reciprocated.

"Everything was incredible, Felicity." Capri shook her head in wonder as she stood near the breakfast buffet the next morning. "I still can't get over you putting an event like that together and during a tropical storm, to boot."

Felicity smiled delicately while she sweetened her coffee. "It's old hat, honey. You'll see."

"Felicity," Capri asked as she filled her plate with eggs and fruit and then moved to the table. "What you said the other day about me being a doctor's wife…"

"Oh, sweetheart, trust me. You'll see when you and Tiberius get married. You'll rush in from the high-profile photography job of yours and put together a dinner party for twenty in the blink of an eye."

Capri gave a prayer of thanks that she didn't choke on her orange juice. "When Tiberius and I get married?"

"Why, yes darlin'." Felicity folded her hands over the cuffs of her pale-blue blouse.

"Felicity, we aren't, I mean…we aren't planning to get married."

"Oh, honey please. Don't tell me that's not in your plans?"

"Well…" Capri rubbed a suddenly clammy hand across the side of her jeans. "It's not in Tibe's plans."

Felicity smiled and added jam to an English muffin. "You just aren't lookin' close enough at that handsome young thing. If you can't see that he is *completely* 'round the bend for you then you're not looking close enough at all."

Capri could only raise her brows and shake her head as Felicity giggled wickedly.

* * *

"Taking some friends out tonight, Doc?" Tiberius was asking Alan Thomas when he found the man on his yacht that morning.

"That was the plan, 'til that monster of a storm rolled in last night."

"Need a hand?" Tiberius offered, pulling himself up on deck.

Alan was already pointing to the bow. "You can tie down that line over there. And then reach in that chest there," he added once Tiberius had completed the first task.

Tiberius grinned when he saw the stash of Heineken filling the chest. "Man after my own heart," he commended and passed the doctor one of the chilled brews.

"Just don't tell Feli," Alan urged with a shudder.

For a brief moment the two colleagues enjoyed the solace on the deck with the chest between them.

"I want to thank you for coming out this weekend, Tiberius. You and that little Capri."

"You're welcome, but we really didn't have a choice. Felicity wouldn't let us leave." Tiberius joined Alan in a round of hearty laughter.

"Congratulations on such a long happy marriage, Doc."

"Hasn't been easy, son." Alan took a swig of the beer. "More years, more work."

Tiberius leaned forward to brace his elbows on his knees. "Can I ask how you manage to keep it going?"

"Communication," Alan drawled and leaned back in the deck chair he occupied. "You gotta stay in each other's faces even when all you want to do is walk away. Takes two people to start an argument and two people to settle one. You gotta be willing to accept your partner's opinions no matter how crazy it makes you."

Tiberius only laughed and enjoyed more of the brew.

Alan kept his gaze focused on the horizon. "When are you gonna do somethin' about changing that cute little thing's last name?"

"Marriage scares me, Doc," Tiberius confessed and massaged his eyes. "What people do to each other when they..."

"Because of your parents?"

"I love her, Doc. I don't want to lose her, but I don't want to hurt her like that. Unfortunately it's all I know. All I've ever seen."

"All you've ever *seen*. Not all you've ever *lived*."

"What's the difference, Doc?"

"A big one, son."

"I'm a jerk when it comes to women."

"She feel that way?"

Tiberius smirked. "If she's smart she does, and she's very smart."

Alan drained the rest of the Heineken. "Well I've seen how she looks at you and she doesn't look at you like you're a jerk. You really want to walk away from that?"

Tiberius wouldn't answer and Alan seemed satisfied by it. The man stood, clapped his younger colleague's shoulder and left him with his thoughts.

Chapter 20

Pepper was shaking her head as she studied the checklist of alcoholic beverages and matched them to the items on hand. "I don't know how you did all this," she marveled and nodded satisfactorily at the brand of rum on the counter. "Finishing up that monstrous project for Tiberius *and* organizing this bachelorette party for Kiva. Prime liquor." She flashed Capri a wink. "As your designated bartender, I commend you."

"Is it really good, Pep?" Capri's expression matched the anxious quality of her voice.

"Hell yes. You know when it comes to parties people often skimp on the brand of liquor. They—"

"Not the booze, Pep, the project. Is it really all right?"

"Jeez." Pepper rolled her eyes. "For the eighth time, yes. I feel like I know Dr. Alan Thomas and I've never even met him. *Very* good work."

Capri let her forehead rest against the table as she sighed. She'd made Pepper view the memory project the second she stepped foot inside her home that day. "I hope Tibe'll think it's good. He doesn't even know I'm done."

Pepper finished with her checklist and turned to look at Capri. She didn't need to ask why Tiberius had no idea the project was complete. Clearly her friend was quite preoccupied about pleasing the beautiful doctor. Pepper couldn't help but wonder how long it would be before there was another bachelorette party in the works.

Next door, Tiberius made a pretense of coming out to look for something in his truck. In truth he was more than a little curious about the two Hummers that had pulled into the driveway behind Capri's and Pepper's cars. When he saw two men jump out of each ride, his curiosity got the better of him and began to heat his temper.

A tiny voice warned him not to pry. An even louder voice demanded that he at least find out what was going on. Tiberius decided to listen to the tiny voice and was glad when he saw three more cars arrive. These were filled with women who parked their vehicles haphazardly across Capri's front lawn. Part of him was a bit miffed that she was having a party and not inviting him, but he shook it off although the curiosity remained.

Kiva's bachelorette party was a screaming success. The twenty two women in attendance enjoyed themselves greatly. They were especially pleased that Capri used a few of her many contacts to score the "entertainment" for the evening.

The male dancers were not only some of Miami's finest, but Capri had created portfolios for several of them. She was in the midst of speaking with a potential subject when one of her guests rushed in to comment on the sexy party favors.

"Take my card and give me a call towards the middle of next week." Capri reached into a small wooden box on the counter where she kept keys and cards. "I'll be on a crazy schedule 'til after my friend's wedding but we'll get you fixed up," she told the model/dancer as she escorted him out of the kitchen.

"Ooo-wee girl! I don't know how you stand it!" Danica Barnes danced in place as she added more chipped ice to the bucket she carried.

"Dani, are you having a good time or playing assistant to Pep?"

"Girl, filling this bucket is the least I can do. You outdid yourself, Cap." She flashed a wink across her shoulder. "Those bodies are prime. Hell, I don't see beauty like that in half the clubs I visit and you know how I love my clubs."

Capri couldn't help but laugh. Danica Barnes's club-hopping was legendary.

"And your late arrival was a sweet touch. *Very* sweet. Just when we thought it couldn't get any better his cute butt comes ringin' the doorbell."

Capri was adjusting the tassels that secured the scoop bodice of her flaring gold dress and only listened absently. "Late arrival?"

Danica poured herself a shot of whiskey. "I know. It was sooo cute how he came over actin' like a concerned neighbor."

Capri tilted her head. "Concerned neighbor?"

"Isn't that the cutest?"

Capri thought she'd be sick if she heard the word *cute* again. But before she could tell that to Danica, Pepper peeked into the kitchen.

"Girl, you might want to get out here," she advised while snapping her fingers toward Danica for the ice bucket.

Capri's eyes widened in surprise and humor, when she walked out into the living room and saw Tiberius surrounded by at least seven adoring women. When he saw her, the look on his face was a cross between terror and relief.

"Cute," Capri had to admit.

Frantically, he began to wave her to his rescue.

"Taking on a second job, Doctor?" she asked once she stood just outside the circle of women.

Tiberius sidestepped the groping hands and moved in behind Capri for protection. Gently yet firmly, he nudged her forward.

"Would you please tell them who I am?"

"Don't they know?"

"Funny." He closed his hands over the cap sleeves of her dress and squeezed. "Tell 'em."

"Sorry girls." Capri struggled to contain her laughter. "This is my neighbor Tiberius Evans. He's not a dancer. He's my actual neighbor."

A round of disappointed groans followed the introduction.

"Come on, Tiberius, we won't tell." Danica tried to press the issue.

"He's also my landlord, Dani."

The ladies were still disappointed but backed away and eventually trickled off in search of new delights. Capri turned to face her "concerned neighbor."

"So just what are *you* doing here?"

Tiberius slanted a soft smile to another passing guest. "I came to see what was going on. What are *you* doing here?"

"This is Kiva's bachelorette party." She nodded at the light clicking on in his head. "The only guys here are strippers, which is what they think *you* are."

Tiberius backed toward the front door. "Capri, I—I'm sorry, um…" He winced at the laughter shimmering in her dark eyes. "I'm just gonna, um, go."

Capri smoothed a hand across his back. "You're more than welcome to stay, but I just can't be responsible for what goes on… or off."

Tiberius uttered a tiny sound of fear. "It's okay, I'll leave. Walk me out?"

"Are you gonna be all right?" She watched him gulp several breaths of night air when they stepped out onto the porch.

"Come see me later?"

The soft-spoken request removed all traces of humor. She only nodded. Tiberius kissed her mouth and sprinted for his house.

As promised, Capri found herself knocking on Tiberius's front door about four hours later. She'd rehearsed the apology she'd come to deliver twice before realizing he wasn't coming to answer the door.

Instead of knocking again, she went around to inspect the back of the house. She found him lounging on his patio and smiled. What her female guests wouldn't have given to see the man as she did just then. Capri's dark gaze was soft as she studied him there, stretched out in nothing but a pair of sleep pants. His massive chest was deliciously bare.

Unable to resist, she strolled over quietly and grazed her fingers across the toned curve of his shoulder. Her breath caught in her throat when his hand snaked out to catch her wrist. A second later she was tugged down softly to straddle his lap. A hard, delicious kiss ensued and she snuggled down more comfortably on top of him. Tiberius's hands roamed and squeezed her thighs as she began to grind upon the rising hardness below his waist. He savored the sudden power behind her kiss and uttered low affected moans in response to the pleasure she provided.

"Where are your girls?" he asked, when their kiss broke for a second.

It took Capri some time to realize who he was talking about.

"Still at my house." She snuggled closer and dropped tiny moist kisses across his jaw. "They're unconscious, but still there."

"So I guess they won't be needing you for a while?" His hand eased beneath the uneven hem of her dress.

Capri tugged at her top lip and shook her head. "Uh-uh, not for a while." She moaned as she felt his fingers inside her panties and then inside of her.

Capri stirred the next morning, cuddled and content in Tiberius's bed. As she slept, he watched her. He'd been awake for quite some time and maintained his spot on the edge of the bed, just studying her as she slumbered. He was recalling his conversation with Alan Thomas. For Tiberius, changing his way of thinking after letting it shape him for a lifetime would be easier said than done. What happened if he was wrong and wound up hurting her as he feared he would? What happened if he did nothing and wound up losing her anyway?

Capri stirred once more and turned to her back as she woke.

"Hey," she purred and stretched like a satisfied feline. Though she was just getting up it wasn't hard to see the pensive emotion tightening Tiberius's features. "You okay?"

"Mmm-hmm." He reached out to smooth the curls from her face.

"Oh, damn!" Capri gasped and bolted up in the bed. Her eyes were wide as she checked the digital clock on the nightstand. "The time. I gotta get home."

Tiberius was already settling her back into bed.

"I need to check on them over there." Capri tried to push back up. Again, she was pushed back into bed. "Tibe, I need to go see them. Especially Kiva. I hope she made it home before dawn or Rod's gonna have a fit and I'll be the one in trouble."

"Listen, I'll check on things over there." He kissed her neck. "I want you to stay," he spoke against her skin.

Capri let her lashes flutter closed. "I don't even know where my clothes are anyway."

"So I guess I've found the perfect way to keep you here, huh?" He cast a wicked glance at the sheet that barely covered her breasts.

"I've gotta go home sometime," she spoke in the midst of a yawn and missed the pained look on Tiberius's face at her mention of leaving.

"Not yet," he whispered when she looked at him. He leaned down to kiss her curls. "Not yet."

Chapter 21

Once Tiberius gave Capri his undying appreciation for the incredible job she'd done on the memory project, he decided a party was in order. Capri complained that she hadn't partied so much even when she lived in the heart of Miami. Still, she eventually warmed to the idea. Another party couldn't hurt, she figured, especially since Tiberius wanted to thank everyone on his committee for all their hard work.

The event was really more of a little appetizer/cocktail party at his home on the evening of Dr. Alan Thomas's retirement gala. A few guests brought dates and Tiberius realized he should have insisted on everyone bringing a friend once he discovered how many of his male colleagues were interested in Capri.

He barely managed to hold his temper when he was cornered by Sam Tremont. The radiologist spent some time raving over Capri— her looks, her work, her looks...

"If I could just talk to her a little more about it."

Tiberius scratched his eyebrow and glanced over Sam's shoulder. "She's still here."

Sam grinned and knocked his fist against Tiberius's arm. "A date is more along the lines of what I had in mind, man."

"What's the point in a date to talk about her work when you can talk to her about it right here?"

"Talkin' about her work isn't all I had in mind."

"Forget it. A date's not gonna happen."

"Aw, Tibe, man, I thought we were boys?"

"We are," Tiberius reciprocated by knocking his fist against Sam's arm and smiling when Sam flinched. "But she's mine."

The appetizers were about to be served when Capri found Tiberius nursing a drink at the rear of the living room.

"Hey? This party was your idea, remember?" She pulled the stout glass from his hand. "*I've* done the bulk of the schmoozing with your colleagues."

Tiberius trailed his fingers along the chiffon sleeve of her gown. "You're really good at that, you know? That schmoozing? There's an art to it, and you've perfected it."

"So I've heard," Capri quipped, as thoughts of Felicity Thomas and her predictions regarding herself and Tiberius came to mind.

"Besides," Tiberius cast a glance around the room, "they're all more interested in speaking to you." He thought about Sam Tremont then.

"Tibe? Are you okay?"

He watched her toying with the knot in his tie and fought the urge to kiss her. "I'm good," was all he managed when she looked up at him.

"Well, they're about to serve appetizers. You may want to eat something. Who knows how long we'll have to wait for dinner when we get to the retirement party?"

"You're right." He put a smile in place, offered her his arm and escorted her toward the appetizers.

Everyone left Tiberius's home for the hospital a little over an hour later. The Ezra C. James Events Gallery at Kelly Memorial was filled almost to capacity. Everyone wanted to be on hand for Dr. Alan Thomas's big night.

Each segment of the evening proved to be a huge success. But it was the photo account of Alan Thomas's remarkable career that stole the show. The account showcased Dr. Thomas's charitable endeavors, of which he was most proud. It was however, the segment featuring the man with his family and friends that the crowd truly enjoyed.

Once the sit-down portion of the event was done, the real celebration began. Tiberius received tons of congratulations on his contribution to the evening. He was quick to tell everyone who the true genius had been. His ease faded when he saw Capri speaking, a little too close for his comfort, with Sam Tremont.

Capri was just handing him her card and telling him to call so they could talk more when Tiberius arrived. Sam didn't even bother to explain and simply raised his hands defensively while he backed away.

Capri's confusion was evident and it took her some time to register Tiberius's offer to dance. She could all but see the tension radiating from his body when he held her. She was grateful for the few times his hold loosened and she was able to take a deep breath.

"Sam." She cleared her throat and focused on the navy blue handkerchief peeking out of the front pocket of his jacket. "Sam's sister is getting married. His wedding gift is to pay for the photography. He's calling next week to discuss it. We've got some fantastic assistants who'd do a great job."

"Did I ask about it, Capri?"

She could feel his chest swell with more tension. "Tibe, it's obvious something's wrong. I thought it might be about Sam. Are you all right?"

"Come on, Capri, how many times will you ask me that?"

"Forget it then," she patted her hand to his chest. "Forget I asked."

They danced only a while longer and then Tiberius was escorting Capri from the dance floor.

"Want a drink?" he asked when they'd returned to their table.

Capri tossed back her hair and fixed him with an agitated stare. "No, why don't you have one? Or a few?"

Tiberius watched as she turned and walked away from him. He

almost went after her but chose the coward's route and headed for the bar. Halfway there, he ran into the guest of honor.

"I can't thank you enough, son."

Tiberius grinned and accepted Alan Thomas's hand to shake. "You're an easy man to honor, sir."

"And where is the lovely Capri? I don't think I've seen you two more than three feet from each other tonight."

Tiberius rolled his eyes. "She's off somewhere, pissed at me."

Alan chuckled and clapped Tiberius's shoulder. "I know you think it isn't safe for a cute li'l thing like that to roam around alone amidst all these dirty old men, but these guys are harmless, you know that."

Tiberius tried to laugh but realized his mentor was serious.

"You need to do something about this, son."

"I'm open to suggestions, Doc." Tiberius massaged the dull ache in his chest.

Alan leaned close. "Stop letting your head rule your heart," he said, and moved on into the crowd.

Chapter 22

Capri pressed the tip of her finger beneath her eye and hoped her mascara wasn't too badly ruined. She and Pepper had just arrived at Rod and Kiva's pre-wedding party. As usual, one of Pepper's off-the-wall remarks had sent Capri into peals of laughter.

"Pep, you can't do this all day," Capri warned, though the laughter coloring her voice made her words sound more playful.

Pepper smoothed her hand over the back of her hair, which was pulled into a high, curly ponytail. "What?"

Capri simply took her hand and looked around at the impressive yacht that had sparked Pepper's humorous comments.

Capri wondered if a yacht would hold all of Rod and Kiva's guests. When she saw the mammoth vessel, her fears were put to rest. The beautiful boat was decorated with white roses and lilies. There was also a huge buffet and a stocked bar on each end. All that, combined with elegantly dressed guests, set a scene that was cool, lovely and undeniably sensual.

"This thing is incredible," Pepper marveled, stepping around Capri to get a better view of the deck. "I don't know where to go first."

"Well, I'm headed in the direction of the buffet table." Capri sighed, rubbing her empty stomach.

Before Capri could make a move toward the food-laden tables, she heard her name being called. She stood looking around the crowded area for a moment, until her dark gaze landed on Tiberius.

Pepper heard the happy sigh Capri uttered and turned to stare at Tiberius as well. He was devastating in a stylish white tux.

Tiberius made his way over to Capri and Pepper, shaking hands with the people he passed on the way. He wore his confidence like a piece of clothing. It was evident in everything he did. Capri pressed her lips together and willed her heartbeat to slow as Tiberius approached them.

Tiberius pressed his hands against the small of Pepper's back and smiled down at her. "How are you, Pepper?"

"Tibe," Pepper exclaimed, smiling into his handsome face, "I guess I don't need to ask how you're doing?"

A small crease formed across his brow. "And why's that?"

"Because you look just fine," Pepper drawled, her gray eyes traveling over Tiberius's tall form.

Capri rolled her eyes as Pepper and Tiberius began to laugh. When Tiberius turned his light-brown eyes toward her, she unconsciously took a deep breath.

"And how are you?"

Capri looked way up to meet his warm, light stare with her darker one. "I'm good," she whispered.

Tiberius enjoyed the sight of Capri standing before his. His intense gaze trailed the form-fitting tangerine spaghetti strapped gown. The eye-catching outfit had a split that reached her mid-thigh, while the bodice gave tantalizing peaks of her full breasts.

"I'm glad you're here," he told Capri, clearing his throat when she noticed his unwavering stare.

Capri smiled. "You know I couldn't miss this. Rod and Kiva are like family."

Tiberius closed his eyes briefly and nodded.

"So, are you nervous about being best man?"

Tiberius shook his head and pressed his hand against his chest. "I just hope I don't lose the ring."

Capri laughed. "I'll bet being in a wedding is the last thing you ever thought you'd do."

A pensive look fell over Tiberius's handsome face. "Nah, it doesn't bother me like it used to," he quietly replied.

Capri was the first to look away. She rubbed her shaky hands over her dress and thought of an escape. "I really need to find that buffet table, I'm starving."

"I know what you mean," he told her, his words holding a special meaning.

Capri smiled and turned away. Pepper had distanced herself a bit, but she still heard the conversation. When Capri walked by and pulled her along, Pepper leaned close.

"Coward," she whispered to her friend.

Amidst all the festivities, Capri and Pepper parted company. Pepper had gone to share a dance with an old boyfriend, while Capri mingled amongst the growing crowd.

The upper deck of the yacht had been designated for the dance area. Capri enjoyed watching several couples grooving to the smooth jazz and R&B coming from the state-of-the-art sound system.

She stood for a while, slowly swaying to the beat of the music. Suddenly, the most delicious caress trailed across her bare back. It traced the smooth skin between her shoulder blades and Capri closed her eyes to enjoy the shivers it sent up and down her spine.

Reluctantly, she opened her eyes and looked behind her. She wasn't surprised to see Tiberius staring down at her.

"I meant to ask you if you heard anything about the photo spread at the retirement gala?" She latched on to the first thing that came to mind.

Tiberius chuckled. "All good things. Don't be surprised if you suddenly have several new clients wanting you to produce their next family reunion or bar mitzvah."

The discussion then surrounded the successful celebration. Capri actually forgot how tense she was and enjoyed herself. Unfortunately, the conversation couldn't last forever and when silence settled, the electricity that always crackled between them simply sparked even more furiously.

Tiberius shifted closer to Capri. Bowing his head, he pressed his mouth next to her ear. "Will you dance with me?"

Without hesitation, Capri placed her hand in his and let him lead her to the dance floor. Laying her head against his shoulder, she breathed in the clean scent of his cologne.

They took advantage of the mellow sounds wafting from the speakers, relishing the opportunity to be so close. Tiberius pressed his face against Capri's soft curls and inhaled the soft perfume of her hair. His large hands smoothed across her back before he slid his arms around her.

"I could stay like this forever." Tiberius spoke softly, but Capri heard every word. She ordered herself not to be taken away by them and tried to laugh off the intensity of the moment.

Undeterred, Tiberius continued. "I think we're on our way to having something worth keeping. Something neither of us wants to lose."

Capri paused and leaned away from him. It was clear that she was completely surprised. She had never expected to hear words like this from Tiberius. "Are you serious?"

"Very." He noticed the lack of certainty in her expression and tilted her chin up with his index finger. "Listen, I'm not trying to push you or anything, but I had to tell you, I…"

"What?"

"That I *am* in love with you. Do you believe me?"

Capri paused again, trying to keep her feet on the ground. She looked up at Tiberius with uncertain eyes.

"Capri, listen. I've known a lot of women, so I know what I'm feeling now is more than anything I've ever felt for anyone else. I'll tell you something else, too, it's scary," he admitted, running a hand through his black hair. "I never intended to get this caught up over *any* woman."

Capri rolled her eyes. "Thanks."

Tiberius shook his head. "Listen, you know why I'm saying that. Other than my grandparents, every marriage or relationship I ever saw in my family ended in divorce or unhappiness. *Every* one— aunts, uncles, cousins… I was just determined not to let it happen to me, I guess. Which is ironic because a romance like my grandparents had is probably the *one thing* I ever really wanted. Maybe it was the fear of failure on my part about this particular aspect of life." He grinned. "That fear was something I could never admit to. I guess I looked at the actions of others and allowed that to make up my mind for me."

"Even now?" Capri asked, not certain where this was going.

"Especially now."

The simple statement and the look in the light-brown depths of his eyes almost drew Capri right in. Still, she resisted the temptation.

Before Tiberius had a chance to continue, the band leader was telling everyone that the wedding ceremony was about to begin.

"You'd better go," Capri whispered, pressing her palms against his chest.

After a moment, Tiberius released her and walked away.

The wedding was like a dream. Rod and Kiva were two people very much in love, and it showed. They'd prepared their own vows, making the ceremony even more special.

Afterward, the party continued. If possible, the scene was livelier than before. While Capri was very happy for her friends, she couldn't help but feel a little down. After the heavy conversation with Tiberius, all she wanted was some clarity. Or at least a good stiff drink.

A while later, Tiberius found Capri seated on a lounge along the patio. He smiled, noticing her nodding off and then shaking herself awake before glancing around to see if anyone had noticed. He decided to shuttle her off to one of the empty cabins aboard the yacht before any of the male guests decided to take advantage of her inebriated state.

As soon as Tiberius lowered her to the bed inside a quiet cabin far away from the music and conversation, Capri began to fidget with the thin straps of her dress. It was obvious that she wanted it off, but was unable to do the job herself.

Tiberius stood staring down at her, wondering if he should help. *Now is the time to prove yourself*, he silently reasoned. Taking a seat on the bed, he gently eased down the straps over her shoulders, then lifted her slightly and unzipped the back. When Tiberius pulled away the gown, his breath caught in his throat at the sight of the strapless white satin bra and matching panties she wore.

He breathed heavily, his gaze taking a leisurely tour over Capri's barely clothed form. Shaking his head, he pulled at the green blanket folded at the foot of the bed. Before covering Capri with it, he bowed his head and pressed a kiss to her forehead.

Sighing, Tiberius made a move to get off the bed. Capri grabbed his jacket lapel.

"Don't go," she whispered.

Tiberius closed his eyes and took a deep breath. He knew Capri was buzzed, yet her softly spoken request was his undoing. Pulling off his jacket, he promised himself he'd only stay until she'd drifted off to sleep.

Tiberius leaned against the headboard and pulled Capri to lie against his chest. He held her for the longest time until he, too, was fast asleep.

Capri awoke later that night with a frown and an aching head. Clearly, she'd had way too much to drink.

What really had her confused though was the chest she was resting against. The hard, muscled surface rose and fell gently beneath her head. Pushing herself up, Capri's eyes widened at the familiar face so close to her own.

"Tibe?"

Tiberius awoke with a jerk, his handsome face darkened by a frown as well. His brown eyes slid over to Capri and the frown was replaced by a sleepy yet satisfied smirk.

"Hello," he slowly greeted.

"What's going on?" Capri surprised herself with the calmness of her voice.

Tiberius yawned and stretched his arms above his head. "What do you think?"

Capri ran one hand through her hair and squeezed her eyes shut. "Tibe...Tibe? Don't you fall asleep on me," she ordered when his eyes began to flutter closed.

Tiberius ran his hands through his hair and pushed himself up in bed. He grimaced at the shallow light and noise coming from out on the deck, signifying the party was still going strong.

"You were pretty much passed out on the deck. I brought you in here. I knew you weren't thinking straight, but you asked me to stay so I did. Nothing happened."

"God." Feeling like a heel, Capri pressed her hand against her forehead. "I'm sorry."

Tiberius shrugged. "Nothing to apologize for. I needed a good nap." He grinned.

Easing closer to him, Capri brushed her hand against the side of his handsome face and leaned over to kiss him. Tiberius immediately moaned at the sweet action and eagerly returned the kiss. Slowly he moved his hands across Capri's bare legs and thighs, pulling her closer, as barely restrained need quickly pummeled through him.

The gasp Capri uttered sounded loud in the quiet cabin. Tiberius effortlessly lifted her across his body. The position allowed Capri to feel the hard length bulging against his trousers.

The kiss became deeper and their moans grew louder. After a

few moments, however, Tiberius broke away and leaned his head back against the headboard.

"What?" Capri asked, a concerned frown clouding her lovely face. She watched Tiberius take several deep breaths with his eyes closed.

"I know what you gave up when you decided to have sex with me. The things that you want, the things that you feel you can never have with a man like me."

Capri smiled and shook her head. "I know what I gave when I decided to sleep with you. It was my decision and it was a decision I'd been struggling with long before I met you." She smiled at the surprise in his eyes. "My decision had a lot to do with the way my sisters handled their own sex lives, or at least the way I *thought* they'd handled them. I knew that same behavior was expected of me, and I didn't want to disappoint anyone." She gave him a refreshing look. "Besides, things being what they are these days, celibacy isn't as surprising a move as it may've been once. I understand what I gave up, Tibe." Her dark gaze was unwavering as she studied his face. "I know what I gave up and it was *my* decision. I did it for me and I did it because I love you." She smiled and squeezed his hand before her gaze faltered. "Wherever that leads us, *if* it leads us, it'll have to be something we both want. No doubts."

They were the words Tiberius most wanted to hear. His eyes trailed over Capri's semi-nude body before his fingers followed the same path. "I don't want to share you, Capri."

Her eyes narrowed playfully. "Share me?"

"I want you. In every way. But I need time. Can you give that to me?"

She scooted closer to him. "Of course I can. I love you. I guess I've been trying to get you to believe me as hard as you've been trying to get me to believe you."

Tiberius pressed his mouth against the base of her neck and

mouthed a soft "thank you" into her skin. While kissing her there, he expertly unfastened her satin bra and tossed it aside. His large hands slid around to cup the full globes for his seeking lips. His mouth worked all over the soft mounds, kissing every inch. Capri ached to feel his lips cover the tip and arched herself closer.

Tiberius surprised her by pushing her back on the bed. His lips then took possession of one firm nipple, manipulating it sensuously. Capri cried out and was soon enthralled by the pleasurable caress. Tiberius let his hands roam freely over her silky-smooth body, stopping at the waistband of her panties.

He slowly traced the outline of the satiny undergarment. One finger traced the fabric covering her womanhood before slipping inside the creamy moisture. Burying his face in the soft crook of her neck, he groaned.

Capri arched her hips so she could feel as much of the caress as possible. She rubbed her foot over Tiberius's long legs encased in the white trousers. The tiny slip of clothing Capri still wore was soon a memory. When she was fully unclothed Tiberius pushed himself up over her and tried to memorize every dip and curve of her body.

Capri tugged at the waistband of his pants, silently relaying her request. Tiberius, however, was way ahead of her. He stood over the bed and removed the rest of his clothes after extracting a condom from the back pocket of his trousers. He pulled Capri off the bed. Kissing her deeply then, he set her against the wall. Capri instantly wrapped her shapely legs around his back as he thrust into her.

The hard length stroking her most sensitive parts had Capri throwing back her head and uttering a loud, lusty cry. Tiberius just buried his face between her breasts as his thrusts became longer and more forceful.

The scene was as beautiful as it was erotic. When they had both reached a place of blissful satisfaction, Tiberius pulled Capri close. They returned to the bed and fell asleep in each other's arms.

Epilogue

Time passed in a blur. Before either Tiberius or Capri realized it, they had invested almost a year-and-a-half in their relationship. They had become exclusive lovers and the closest of friends.

They even made it through the birth of their dogs' puppies. Droopey and Lewey became the proud parents of twelve black puppies. Everyone who saw them was determined to have one of their own.

Capri couldn't remember when she'd been so happy. Not only had she found a wonderful lover, she had also found an even more wonderful friend. Of course they both aggravated each other immensely at times but the relationship grew stronger in the midst of it all.

One evening, Capri arrived home to find a note taped to her door. It was an invitation from Tiberius for an eight-o'clock dinner at his home. Capri wasn't surprised. If she wasn't at Tiberius's place, he was at hers. Of course, there were no complaints from either side.

Rushing into her house, she took a quick shower and changed. Her sky-blue, form-fitting frock flared around her knees. It had cap sleeves, an upturned collar, and a row of tiny buttons that reached her middle. Several were left undone to reveal teasing glimpses of her chest. The ensemble was completed by a pair of flat sling-back sandals and was perfect for a casual evening.

The instructions on Tiberius's note told her to enter through the gate and she did so. Her dark eyes widened in surprise when she saw the delicious spread on a cart next to a small round table for two. There were marinated grilled chicken breasts, steamed rice with a rich butter sauce, vegetables, and a gorgeous green salad.

White wine and strawberry shortcake rounded out the light, beautiful meal.

Capri's smile widened when she noticed that the pool was lit. Walking closer, she knelt to test the water, which was surprisingly warm to the touch. Overhead, she could hear the smooth sultry sounds of Diana Krall singing a sensuous tune.

For a long moment, Capri just stood marveling at how lovely everything was. After a while she felt a soothing caress across her bare arms. Turning, she slid her hands across Tiberius's chest encased in a short-sleeved tan cotton-knit shirt. Her lips instantly parted when Tiberius dipped his head and pressed his mouth against hers.

They both moaned as their tongues fought a heated duel in the lusty kiss. Capri arched her small voluptuous frame against Tiberius's hard body as her hands roamed his back. Tiberius squeezed his eyes shut tighter. His arousal reached a fevered pitch. Before he could become too sidetracked, he pulled himself away and bowed his head.

"What is it?" Confusion tugged Capri's brow.

Tiberius didn't answer, but took her hand and led her to the patio. "Do you want a drink before dinner?" he asked, after helping her into a seat.

Slowly, Capri shook her head. "I'm fine for now."

Tiberius pushed one hand through his hair and another into the back pocket of his beige cotton slacks. "Capri, at the risk of saying something you're never gonna believe…"

Capri's dark eyes widened expectantly and she tilted her head. "Yes?"

Tiberius winced and began to pace the floor.

Capri would've laughed had Tiberius's face not held such a serious look. Instead, she leaned forward in her chair and set her hands atop the table. "Why don't you take a minute and—"

"No…no I've already waited long enough to say this as it is. And I think you've waited long enough on me."

Capri relaxed. "What are you doing?"

A dimple appeared in Tiberius's cheek as he smiled. "I'm doing a bad job of proposing to you."

Realization dawned in Capri's eyes. She sat up straighter in her chair. "Proposing?"

"That is, if you haven't gotten tired of waiting for me?"

"Waiting?" Capri couldn't force herself to do more than utter one-word questions.

Tiberius shook his head. "Will you marry me, Capri?"

Capri closed her eyes and for a moment Tiberius thought she'd fainted. Relief washed over him when they fluttered back open. "Marry?"

Tiberius knelt beside her chair. "Now's the time for answers, not questions." He smiled. "So may I have one?"

"Tibe…"

He stood then, leaning against the small dinner table and pulling Capri against him. Patting the small of her back, he settled his lips against her ear. "Marry me?"

Capri gasped and pulled away when she felt him slide something round and dazzling on her finger. She stared at the sparkling piece of jewelry for a moment, before her eyes snapped to his.

At first Capri could only nod. Then, the words began to spill from her lips. "Yes, yes, yes…"

"I love you," Tiberius told her simply, his warm brown eyes intense with emotion.

Again, Capri nodded. "I love you."

Tiberius cleared his throat in a playful manner. "Are you only saying that because I was your first?" Tiberius joked.

Capri smiled but decided to offer up a serious answer. "At first," she finally admitted, "maybe it's why I was so afraid of admitting my own feelings. I knew having sex would be a big factor and I didn't want it to be the only reason and at first it was. I couldn't admit that to myself then."

Tiberius pressed a kiss to her forehead. "I guess we both had some lessons to learn."

"You're right."

"You know," Tiberius sighed, as he gathered her closer in his arms, "it's weird. I spend so many days talking to couples about to become parents—advising them on how to work with their partner, understand where they're coming from, how they're coping with changes that are taking place in their lives, but I never realized how much all that pertained to me and what was going on in my own mind."

"How much it pertains to *us*." Capri savored the kiss he gave her. "I'd say we both had a lot going on in our minds."

"Well, my mind's made up, and I know I love you with every bit of it."

"Every bit of my mind," Capri reciprocated and nuzzled his cheek with her nose. "Every bit of my body."

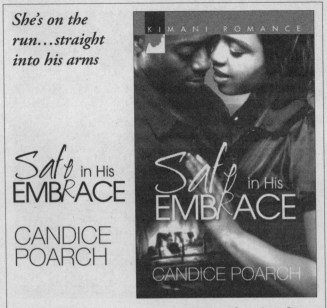

REQUEST YOUR FREE BOOKS!

2 FREE NOVELS
PLUS 2 FREE GIFTS!

KIMANI ROMANCE™

Love's ultimate destination!

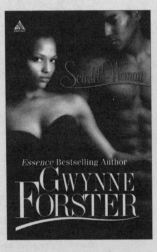